China Code

Books by Matthew J. Flynn

Bernie Weber: Math Genius Series
Book 1: Milwaukee Jihad
Book 2: China Code

Coming Soon!
Book 3: Hunting Bernie Weber

China Code

Communist Chinese Assassination Squad;
Math Genius Target on the Run;
Gangs of Milwaukee Take Them On

Matthew J. Flynn

SPEAKING VOLUMES, LLC
NAPLES, FLORIDA
2023

China Code

ISBN 978-1-64540-899-4

Chapter One

"To our leader, Comrade Yan Shifan," toasted Chinese General Li Yu and three other generals as they sat facing the portrait of the president of China. "May his wise counsel continue to guide our country."

"To our leader," murmured the other officers, who were gathered together in the counterintelligence room of the Ministry of State Security.

"Comrades, I have wonderful news."

Li Yu showed emotion, a rare and unpleasant sight in a Chinese flag officer.

"One of our mathematicians has proven the Riemann hypothesis. The most difficult problem in all mathematics."

"Beyond belief!" exclaimed a comrade.

"In the process," Li Yu said, "he also discovered an algorithm to encrypt our communications in a new manner that will prevent the Americans from deciphering our traffic. And the Americans will never be able to decode it."

"Magnificent. And the mathematician. He was Han?"

Li Yu stopped smiling and stared at the floor.

"No, Comrade," he said hesitantly. "He was Uighur."

There was a painful silence.

"Comrades, I have a solution. We will not publish his results, and the world will never know. We will use the results only for our own advantage in cryptology. But of course, the genius who discovered the solution must be Han. He must be a member of the Chinese race."

"And who will it be, Comrade Li Yu?"

"Professor Yin Hou. I have spoken with him, and he will accept the honor. If it ever becomes public, he will also do so publicly for the rest of the world."

"Does he understand and accept the conclusions of the Uighur man?"

"The Uighur boy. He is just sixteen years old. Yes, after some study, Professor Yin Hou understands the proof."

"But the boy, comrade. What about him?"

"He will be told he will be given a prize granted to him by the leader. The boy will receive the Lei Feng medal for service to the Chinese military, and he and his parents will board a military plane in Xinjiang at Urumqi. There will be nine people on board when it takes off: the boy, his parents, two pilots, and four soldiers of our counterinsurgency commando team. When the plane lands in Beijing, there will only be six passengers onboard, and they will be met by Professor Yin Hou. A private ceremony will be conducted honoring Yin Hou."

The other generals smiled and raised their glasses.

"To Professor Yin Hou," said one. "And to our leader, Yan Shifan. May his wisdom guide our nation."

Chapter Two

A teenage boy, his parents, and four soldiers stood near a plane.

"We are so proud of both our son and our leader," said his father. "We'll show that we are loyal Chinese citizens. We can help to defend our nation. The actions of a few of us are denounced by most Uighurs."

"Congratulations, Comrade," said one of the soldiers. "It is time to depart."

The man and his wife and son boarded first, followed by the soldiers. The two pilots were already seated in the cockpit. The ground crew waved the small jet to the runway for takeoff. Rising sharply at a steep angle, the plane disappeared into the clouds as it headed eastward.

One hour later, a woman tilling her field paused to wipe her forehead. She heard a faint noise in the distance. A scream. A human scream? The woman stood still. There were no further sounds. She shrugged and resumed her work.

Finally, the jet began its approach to Beijing and landed on a side runway. A small delegation stood waiting for them. When the four soldiers came down the stairway, the commander shook hands with an elderly man standing at the base of the stairs.

"Professor Yin Hou?" the commander said.

The elderly man bowed his head.

"Congratulations, Professor. We will escort you to the award ceremony."

The man bowed his head again. They all got into a waiting limousine and drove away. As soon as they left, a janitor boarded the plane. The two pilots were still in their seats, finishing their paperwork. Nobody else was aboard the aircraft.

Chapter Three

My name is Joe Weber, and I have a B.A. in political science from Milwaukee Community College. I am currently unemployed. You've got to understand something about me and my family. My mom told me that when I was a baby, I drank my bottle by holding it in my feet. She said I did it so that I could count my toes. And I'm the least compulsive person in my family. We're all good at math, specially my nephew Bernie.

I'll never forget the day I was walking up to the student union of the University of Wisconsin in Madison with my girlfriend, Frannie Ferraro. Bernie was one of the four finalists in a national math competition. He's a math major at Milwaukee Community College. The finals were held in the UW-Madison Union's Rathskeller.

Frannie was a teaching assistant in Spanish at Milwaukee Community College. We were there that day to cheer on Bernie.

You need to understand something about Milwaukee. We're different from everyone else. We're disturbingly literal. Many Milwaukeeans think that tact is something you eat. That nuance is a perfume.

For instance, if you showed someone from Milwaukee a picture of your newborn baby with big eyes and a beautiful smile, he would say, "What large eyes he has! Have you had his thyroid checked?"

Or a Milwaukeean will say, "Your best friend died in a fire? I'm so sorry! Did he change the batteries in his smoke detector?"

Milwaukee is suspicious of anyone who appears to live well. The headline in a recent article of *The Milwaukee Journal* about a recluse who hid out in the Maine woods for twenty-five years by stealing food from empty cabins read "Hermit Lives High End Lifestyle." This wasn't satire. The article hit him for stealing brand names and ignoring generics.

The truth is that everyone's nose in Milwaukee is deeper into your business than in any town in the entire United States. We notice everything. Our newspaper is partly to blame. The *Journal* searches out the unworthiness of everything in the city. When a Milwaukee kid starred on the UW Football team and was up for the NFL draft, *The Milwaukee Journal* reported it:

FALLING SLOWLY

"Wisconsin's August Schmidt will be the slowest NFL football player in a generation. The farther he goes, the worse he looks. When he lurched down the surface of the combine in the forty, he was painful to watch. As one executive said, 'He's not a good athlete, but I didn't think he'd run this slow.' Said another, 'The workout exposed him; his feet are so bleeping slow. He's beginning to scare me the more I watch him.' "

Madison is only seventy-five miles away, but it's very different from Milwaukee. Madison's a reef of small organisms that grew up to protect each other from the universe. The water is cold outside the reef, and food is scarce. Inside the reef, food is plentiful, and the water is balmy, protected from storms. Politics bursts from people's eyeballs as you walk past them on the street.

There was a crowd around the Union holding signs as we approached.

RECALL RIDER!

RIDE HIM OUT OF TOWN!

INDICT RIDER!

Todd Rider is the governor, a Republican. He was speaking at the math competition.

The demonstrators were a mixed crowd, mostly teachers and office workers, but also a lot of old timers who stumble out of East Washington and Williamson Streets to recapture their past whenever they hear there's political action going on.

On the fringes of the crowd, an old man with matted hair—a Nixon-era relic left over from the 1960s—held up a sign that said, MATH KILLS/MATH = WAR!

Someone in the early 1970s actually blew up the Math Research Center at Madison because it was doing research for the military. The blast killed some guy. You still see some of these older cats hanging around the Union for the cheap coffee, like the Japanese soldiers who hid in the Philippines after World War II and lived in caves.

It was just a few minutes before the opening ceremony. The governor was already sitting on the stage at the Rat as Frannie and I slid into two seats on the side in the front. A Chinese guy with a laptop was sitting by himself across the aisle. At the time, I didn't pay him any attention.

A man in a tweed jacket with patches on the elbows said, "Ladies and Gentlemen. Would you please take your seats."?

He tapped a gavel.

"Thank you. I am Professor Ogden Fethers of Yale University. It gives me great pleasure to preside over the Gibbs Math Competition that is held annually among colleges in the United States. But first, I would like to introduce Wisconsin governor Todd Rider, who will officially welcome us to Wisconsin. Governor?"

Todd Rider, the policy mule for the billionaire, out-of-state Weed brothers, pranced up to the podium. He had been elected governor because the Weeds had pumped $30 million into his campaign. His job was to vacuum cash out of public assets and sweep it into the brothers' pockets.

The Weeds weren't alone. Two hedge funds that wanted to milk the public employees' pension fund also bought time shares in Rider.

Even with the money, Rider was so bad he almost lost. A former staffer for a nonprofit, he never had an original idea. But the Weeds and the hedge funds bought him a copy of Cliff's Notes for Ayn Rand's novels to give him an intellectual patina. They brought him to Hedge Fund Candidate School on Broad Street in New York, where he learned to speak with feigned candor about anything his donors whispered to him.

Rider slipped into office.

"Thank you. Thank you, Professor Fethers," Rider said.

I have to hand it to Rider. He looks like a cherub, or a choir member casting saintly glances at the heavens while he sings from a hymnal. But he has a *Village of the Damned* sheen to his eyes. This sort of guy gives me the shivers.

"I'm pleased to be here at this Math event," Rider continued. "Counting is what separates us from the lower order of creatures. For instance, the Democrats attack me for turning down money from the federal government to run trains through Wisconsin from Chicago to Minneapolis. But they can't cipher. What possible good could it do for Wisconsin to be connected to Chicago and Minneapolis? To the Bears and the Vikings? Go Packers!"

Rider rambled until he was hustled off the stage by his handlers to tepid and relieved applause.

Ogden Fethers tapped his gavel lightly.

"It now gives me great pleasure to introduce our four finalists in the Gibbs Math Competition. Some of the previous winners have made important contributions to mathematics."

He paused to sip some water. My nephew, Bernie, was sitting on the left, dressed in a sweater and khaki pants. He stared solemnly at the audience. Bernie had bushy, light brown hair, and plump cheeks, and he looked younger than his nineteen years. Frannie waved at him. Bernie smiled but didn't wave back.

"First, I'd like to introduce Mr. Stuart Miller of Columbia University."

A kid in a sport coat wearing aviator glasses waved from the seat next to Bernie.

"Stuart attended the Bronx High School of Science prior to enrolling at Columbia and is planning a career as a mathematics professor."

The crowd applauded.

"Next, I'd like to introduce Ms. Emily Mathews of MIT."

A pretty girl with a ponytail waved. She was wearing a simple black dress with an accenting pink scarf.

"Emily prepared at Elmhurst Academy and plans to start her own software company."

The crowd applauded again.

"Next, please welcome Mr. Basil Tawney of Yale University. Basil prepped at Andover, like his father, and intends to start his own hedge fund."

The crowd clapped.

Basil was also wearing a tweed jacket but without leather patches.

"Basil is a legacy, and we are quite proud of him. He is the son of Kingman Tawney, Yale Class of 1983, and the grandson of Rutherford "Rusty" Tawney, Yale Class of 1953."

The crowd saw no need to clap again.

"And finally, we also welcome Mr. Bernie Weber of Milwaukee Community College."

Fethers glanced again at his notes.

"Mr. Weber went to Riverside High School in Milwaukee, a public school. We congratulate him on his accomplishment in even getting this far, and I'm certain that he appreciates being at an event like this. He doesn't know yet what he wants to do, but he says he likes math. When he was in high school, Bernie performed in a math circus as a math rapper named Mr. Pryme Knumber. I believe he wore a cape and fake green ears."

Fethers chuckled.

"He says he likes prime numbers. Bernie, son, I bet you're just pinching yourself at being here, right?"

"Yeah. Kinda."

"What I mean, Bernie, it that it's almost beyond belief that you are here and competing against this field. Are you nervous?"

"Not really."

Frannie glared at Fethers. She stuck two fingers in her mouth. Her whistle could have cracked a glass. Fethers glared back but said nothing.

"All right," Fethers went on. "Contestants, we are giving you four problems. You have five minutes each to solve the first two. You may use the calculators you have been given, or paper and pen, but no laptops or other equipment. No help from the audience either. Understood?"

The students all nodded.

"It's sudden death. If you get an answer wrong, you leave the stage."

They nodded again.

"You will be given ten minutes to solve the third problem, and the fourth problem requires you to write a proof of a hypothesis. You will be graded on the elegance of your response. Understand? Here's your first problem."

Fethers moved a mouse, and a text lit up on a screen.

The following are four conjectures. One of them is false. Identify the false conjecture, the one that has been disproven.

Four Conjectures

1. Every integer greater than seventeen is the sum of three *distinct* prime numbers.

2. There is an infinite number of twin primes. A twin prime is a prime number that differs from another prime by two, such as forty-one and forty-three.

3. There is an infinite number of Cullen primes, expressed as n-2n+1, or Cn.

4. Fifty percent or more of the natural numbers less than any given number have an odd number of prime factors.

"All right, you may begin."

Bernie yawned and slouched back in his chair. Fethers looked at him.

"Mr. Weber. You only have four minutes left."

"That's Okay. I wrote my answer down."

"Then you may want to recheck it."

"Thank you."

Bernie didn't move. Fethers finally called time.

"Okay, our panel of three mathematicians will now inspect the responses. I call on Professor Leo Lettow of the University of Wisconsin to collect the answers."

Lettow bounded over to the students. He was exceptionally lean, almost gaunt. As a matter of fact, I've never seen a fat UW prof after the budget cuts.

Lettow and two other professors examined the answers, and then Lettow whispered to Fethers.

"Congratulations to each of the contestants," Fethers said. "Every student got this one right. The answer is number four, the conjecture about fifty percent or more of the natural numbers. It was proposed by Polya in 1919 and disproved by Haselgrove in 1958."

He gestured at the screen.

"The other three have never been disproved and are almost certainly true. Now we'll proceed to the second problem."

Fethers moved the mouse once again:

Epigraph on the Tomb of Diophantus

This tomb holds Diophantus. God granted him to be a boy for the sixth part of his life, and, adding a twelfth part to this, he clothed his cheeks with down. He lit him the light of wedlock after a seventh part, and five years after his marriage, he granted him a son. But after attaining the measure of half his father's life, chill Fate took him. After consoling his grief by this science of numbers for four years, Diophantus ended his life.

Ogden Fethers pointed to the screen.

"The great Diophantus of Alexandria gave us Diophantine equations. We thought we'd have a little fun and decipher his epigraph. The question: How old was Diophantus when he died, and how old was his son?"

I was glad he didn't expect me to answer it. Bernie yawned. He wrote on his pad, sat back, and folded his arms. The other three wrote furiously, occasionally looking up at the screen.

"Okay, time," said Fethers.

Lettow scrambled around to collect the answers. Fethers frowned as he read them.

"I'm sorry to say that we have our first casualty. The correct answer is that Diophantus was eighty-four when he died, and his son was forty-two. Three students got it right. Basil, I'm afraid your answer was eighty-six and forty-three."

Basil Tawney shrugged and left the stage.

Fethers clicked the mouse again.

"Here's the third problem. The snowplow problem. You'll have ten minutes to solve this one. It should appeal to my friends here in Wisconsin, who get a lot of snow."

The screen said: **The Snowplow Problem**

One morning it starts to snow at a constant rate. Later, at six a.m., a snowplow sets out to clear a straight street. The plow can remove a fixed volume of snow per unit time. Its speed is inversely proportional to the depth of the snow. If the plow covered twice as much distance in the first hour as the second hour, what time did it start snowing?

What, the driver wore a red shirt, so what did he have for breakfast? What was this? I pitied the other two students, but I had full faith in Bernie. If anybody could make something of this dog's breakfast, it was Bernie.

He put his pen down after about five minutes and sat back. The other two scribbled until Ogden Fethers called time.

"All right, once again I will ask Professor Lettow to collect the answers."

Lettow collected the three papers before huddling with his two colleagues. I could see them arguing with each other, and then they called Fethers over to speak with them.

Carrying the three papers, Fethers finally returned to the podium.

"The panel and I have decided that we have one casualty, while two students remain in the competition. The correct answer is that it started snowing at five twenty-two and fifty-five seconds in the morning. One student got that right. Mr. Weber, congratulations. That was very impressive. But another student, Ms. Mathews, wrote five twenty-three in the morning. Because we were not precise about rounding, we assume that was rounding, and we also accept that answer."

The crowd applauded Bernie and Emily.

"Mr. Miller, your answer of five thirty in the morning was a valiant effort, and we wish you much success in your career."

Poor Miller slunk off into the back of the room, leaving Bernie and Emily Mathews. The Chinese guy chuckled across the aisle.

"And now for the final question," Fethers said. "Here I must add that I, Professor Lettow, and our colleagues decided we would permit ourselves a little adventure—a small experiment. Have a little fun. We'll give you the most difficult hypothesis in all of mathematics and ask you to prove it: The Riemann Hypothesis. It was proposed in 1859 by Bernhard Riemann in Germany, and no one has ever proven or disproven it. Among other things, its proof would have profound implications for cryptography."

Ogden Fethers paused to survey the crowd.

"And for the family and supporters of Mr. Weber and Ms. Mathews, I want to explain our thinking. Of course, we don't expect a student to prove or disprove a hypothesis that the best mathematicians in the world have failed to solve in more than 160 years. But by presenting it as an ambush problem to two unsuspecting and very bright and enthusiastic young minds, we want to see if they have a flash of insight that can contribute to the solution. We will grade their efforts and award the prize to the one with the most original insight."

Fethers clicked the mouse for the final round:

Prove or Disprove the Riemann Hypothesis

The Riemann hypothesis states as follows: ALL NON-TRIVIAL ZEROS OF THE ZETA FUNCTION HAVE REAL PART ONE-HALF. It is described in a three-page handout that you will be given before the time period starts. Briefly stated, the prime numbers decline in frequency the higher you go. There are 25 prime numbers between one and one hundred. But there are only 4 prime numbers in the last block of 100 numbers before one trillion. We think they keep thinning out the higher you go, although they are infinite. Why? Why do they thin out like that?

How are they distributed? A proof of the Riemann hypothesis might give us the answer.

"You will have one-half hour to submit your answer."

I walked around the room as Professor Lettow gave Bernie and Emily Mathews their handouts. Some people in the audience stretched and visited with each other, while others argued about the questions and the solutions. The Chinese man typed steadily on his laptop.

I stepped outside. The demonstrators had gone. I walked over to the foot of Bascom Hill and looked over the lawn and up at the statute of Abraham Lincoln. It was a lovely spring afternoon. The trees on Bascom Hill were all budding. The lawn was filled with students reading on blankets or curled up on the grass. Abe sat in his chair, eternally watching over the university, looking out into the distance toward the Capitol.

When I went back inside, time was almost up. Bernie had finished and Emily Mathews was still writing.

"All right, Mr. Weber. Ms. Mathews. Time's up. Professor Lettow, please collect their answers."

Lettow took their sheets of paper. He showed them to his two colleagues. They read in silence for the next several minutes as they passed the papers to one another. Then they spoke heatedly, although it could have been from excitement, and Lettow hurried over to Fethers to consult with him.

As he joined them, Fethers was handed one of the answers, and the others remained quiet while he read. Finally, the four of them resumed an intense conversation, before Fethers walked slowly back to the podium, holding the answers.

"Ladies and gentlemen. If I can please have your attention. We have a winner. I must also say that the answer from this student has far exceeded our expectations."

"But first, I would like to congratulate our second-place finisher for a remarkable insight into a most difficult problem. Would Ms. Emily Mathews please step forward and join me at the podium."

Mathews walked over to join him, her lip quivering but managing a smile.

"Ms. Mathews, your answer showed keen insight. In acknowledging the decreasing frequency of the primes, you showed that their frequency is inversely proportionate to the logarithm. Although it's been proven before, for a student to deduce it so short a time and under pressure is an excellent performance. Well done, and congratulations on winning second place."

Mathews and Ogden Fethers shook hands.

"And now, will Mr. Bernie Weber step forward, please?"

Bernie joined Fethers at the podium.

"Mr. Weber, I'm not certain how to put this, but your performance can only be described as extraordinary—quite extraordinary."

Thunderous applause erupted from the audience. Hooting and whistling, Frannie jumped out of her seat.

"Thank you, ladies and gentlemen."

Fethers kept quiet until the applause died down.

"Bernie, while you didn't prove the hypothesis, what you did prove was a portion of it that went beyond existing advances."

He looked out at the audience.

"Bernie proved that an infinite number of the zeta function's non-trivial zeros satisfy the RH. That is, that they have real part one-half. "

The Chinese guy was now typing madly.

"I know that sounds like gibberish to many of you in this audience," said Fethers, "but to put it in perspective, this also was proven by a mathematician named Hardy in 1914 after a great deal of effort. But

Bernie proved it in a different way. His insight opens a new approach to proving the hypothesis! Bernie, well done young man!"

Frannie and I stood back while Bernie was congratulated by many in the audience. The Chinese guy jumped the line to get close to Bernie, who shook his hand.

"Very good," the man said. "Very interesting accomplishment. I would like to stay in contact with you."

He handed Bernie a card.

"Could we talk about your work?"

"I'll tell you what," I said, taking the card and putting it in my pocket. "I'm Bernie's uncle. No need to contact us. If we need to contact you, we'll know where to find you. Thanks."

The man bowed his head stiffly. He pulled out his phone and dialed as he walked away.

"Can we interrupt you to have Bernie up here for a picture?" said Fethers.

"Sure. Bernie, what do you want to do later? Pizza at Paisan's?"

"That'd be excellent," Bernie said.

As Frannie and I waited for Bernie, I saw an attractive woman in her mid-thirties pull out her phone. She stood in the corner talking quickly with her back to everyone. I paid no more attention to her at the time.

Chapter Four

The phone rang at seven in the morning in the kitchen of an apartment on Lianshi Lu Street near the International Sculpture Park in Beijing. A man was eating breakfast at a small table by himself. He picked up the phone.

"*Wei.*"

"Comrade, I must speak with you."

"Where are you calling from?"

"The University of Wisconsin."

The man paused.

"What is the province of your mother's mother?"

"Guizhou Province, Comrade."

"The province of my mother's mother?"

"Guangxi Province."

"Proceed."

In a corner of the UW Rathskeller, the man spoke rapidly in Chinese. Most of the audience had already left. When the caller finished, the man on Lianshi Lu street was silent for a moment before he spoke.

"Did he solve the hypothesis? Prove it?"

"Of course not. Not in half an hour. But he proved a portion of it in a new way. Like the first step in Professor Yin Hou's solution."

Another pause.

"I will inform the group. We will meet to discuss this. You will join us by phone."

"Yes, Comrade."

"In the meantime, copy the boy's transcripts. Course descriptions. Send us the textbooks he used in them. Do so today."

"Yes, Comrade."

"And send us a copy of his answer. Immediately."

"Yes, Comrade."

"*Bai bai.*"

"*Zai Jian.*"

Chapter Five

The woman in the corner tapped her foot impatiently as the phone rang.

"Hello?" someone said.

"I need to talk with Maynard."

"Who is this?"

"Audrey."

"The present population of the town where you were born?"

"10,918."

"Just a minute."

The woman looked back into the room. The contestants had already left.

"Hello?"

"Maynard? I need to talk to you."

"Where are you?"

"The UW student union. The competition just got done."

"Why are you calling?"

She whispered urgently into the phone.

"He did this in half an hour?"

"You wouldn't believe it."

"Wait a minute. This is the Weber kid? The same kid we chased around Milwaukee a few years ago?"

"Right. I wasn't involved in that. But that's what I understand."

"Get a copy of his answer. And come home. I will see you tomorrow afternoon. Goodbye."

Chapter Six

General Li Yu looked around the table as he reached for the speaker phone.

"Are we ready?"

The four other men at the table nodded. Two wore military uniforms. Professor Yin Hou and another man wore suits. General Li Yu pressed a button.

"Comrades, we will now hear a description of what occurred in Wisconsin. Our comrade in Madison who observed the competition is on the line. You may proceed."

"I attended the final mathematics competition, as instructed. It was amusing at first. A multiple-choice question, and several problems. But then the finalists were instructed to solve the Riemann hypothesis."

Yin Hou chuckled into the phone.

"Absurd. Students at a competition? In what time?"

"Half an hour. It was stated that they were not expected to solve it. The professors were looking for flashes of insight."

"And the result?"

"A girl from MIT reported a trivial insight that was discovered long ago. The relation to the logarithm. She may have simply repeated her coursework. But the boy from Wisconsin disturbs me."

"For what reason?"

"He proved Hardy's result. But his method was different from Hardy's. His method was the one that . . . you discovered. Properly applied, it will lead to the final proof. And that proof will yield the algorithms that are the basis of our cryptology."

There was silence as the men in Beijing looked at General Li Yu.

"We have studied his academic background," the general finally said. "He has no history with the problem. No course he has ever taken even mentions it. You believe that he did all this in half an hour with no advance notice?"

"Yes."

"Very well. Here are your instructions. I will send a team to Wisconsin. You will lead it. Follow him at every moment. Monitor all his conversations. Determine if he shows further interest in the problem. If he does, we will invite him to China at our expense. To receive . . . an award."

Those at the table chuckled.

"He will receive the Lei Feng medal for outstanding mathematical work by . . . someone under twenty-five."

"A new award?"

"Yes. A new award. We will determine whether the threat is serious."

"And if it is?"

"We will do what is necessary to protect China."

"What if he does not accept our invitation?"

"We will bring him here anyway."

"May the wisdom of Yan Shifan guide our nation."

"It will be so."

Chapter Seven

A woman knocked on the door of a Georgetown townhouse. She waited until a buzzer sounded to let him in.

"May I help you?"

A middle-aged woman with her hair in a bun, wearing a blouse buttoned to the throat, sat at a small desk in the middle of the foyer. The walls of the room were painted sienna red. The mantle of the fireplace and two tables held vases with fresh flowers. A large Oriental rug with a picture of a sultan and four peacocks covered much of the floor.

"I'm Audrey. I have an appointment with Maynard Gieck."

"He's expecting you. They're upstairs in the conference room."

The woman walked up the walnut spiral staircase and stood at the open door of a conference room. Four men sat at the table. One of them waved her in.

"Gentlemen, I'd like you to meet Audrey Knapp. I told you about our conversation. Audrey is one of my mathematicians at NSA. Audrey, this is Lathrop Willis, who you met before. He's director of operations for the other agency."

Gieck gestured toward an elderly man with a full head of white hair. Willis sat frowning with his arms folded. He didn't acknowledge the woman's nod.

"And this is Carroll Dalton, director of research."

Gieck pointed toward the man next to Willis. Dalton was heavy, plump by Wisconsin standards, morbidly obese by any other. He nodded and stared at Audrey, never blinking.

"And this is Wayne Hawkin, associate director of operations," Gieck said, waving toward the third man. Hawkin nodded impatiently.

"Tell us what happened."

Audrey smoothed her skirt. She was an exceptionally good-looking woman in her mid-thirties with large, blue eyes. She wore her thick, auburn hair clipped back.

"I found it hard to believe. Of course, we monitor all math competitions. The finals."

"Were the Chinese there?" said Gieck.

"Yes. I didn't recognize this one."

"Go ahead."

"The finalists had to solve four problems. One on prime-number conjectures. And two other problems. Medium difficulty. Two of them solved them."

"And then?"

"And then they were asked to solve the Riemann Hypothesis."

"What kind of BS is that? They weren't told the problems in advance, right?"

"Well, right. The moderator said they weren't expected to solve it. He said they were looking for a possible insight. Basically, since we're at a dead end on it and no one's proven it in a long time, why not see if some flash occurs to bright kids looking at it for the first time."

"And what happened?"

"The student from MIT actually did an amazing job. She proved the relation to the logarithm. That was proven before, but I don't think she'd studied it. She seemed to arrive at it independently."

"And how about the boy from Wisconsin? Bernie Weber. The kid from Milwaukee."

"Wait a minute."

Willis held up his hand.

"Just to confirm. This is the same kid who did the prime numbers in his head. Whom we had so much trouble with in Milwaukee."

"Right," Gieck said. "So what did he do this time, Audrey?"

"It was beyond amazing. He proved that an infinite number of the zeta function's non-trivial zeros satisfy the hypothesis."

"Didn't Hardy prove that a hundred years ago?"

"Sure. But this kid in Wisconsin took a totally new approach to the proof. We got a copy of his answer, and I looked at it. The hypothesis isn't my specialty, but what he did opens up lines of attack on the problem I'd never heard before."

"Look, what am I missing here?" Hawkin said. "If they proved that there are infinite numbers that satisfy this hypothesis a hundred years ago, that means it's proved, right?"

"No. There could also be infinite numbers that violate it."

"*What?*"

"Look," said Audrey. "There is an infinite number of infinities. Like take the even numbers two, four, six, eight and so on. They're infinite, right? Go on forever?"

"Right."

"And the odd numbers are the same, right? One, three, five, seven, nine and so on?"

"Right."

"Then how about both numbers together—one, two, three, four, five, and so on? They're infinite, too. And they're the odd and even combined. Are there more of them than just the even? Or the odd?"

"Yes!" Hawkin said. "I mean no! Yes."

"I've heard enough."

Willis waived dismissively.

"Hawkin, you and I don't do math. We do history. We hire people who do math. Audrey, our thanks for your good work. You're excused."

They waited until she closed the door and left.

"All right," Willis said. "First of all, what's Audrey's background? Is she solid? Is this for real?"

"Absolutely," said Gieck. "BA Boston College, PhD at NYU. Did her dissertation on some problems in number theory. She's worked for me for five years. First-rate mathematician."

"All right. Gentlemen, I'd like to hear from Maynard first on the problem itself, and then from Dalton on the Chinese connection. Then you're excused. Hawkin and I will discuss further action. Maynard."

"Right."

Gieck lowered a screen. He clicked to the first slide. It showed a man in clothes from the 1800s, round, receding hairline, with small, wire-rimmed glasses and a bushy, black beard.

"This is Bernhard Riemann. German mathematician. Died at age thirty-nine in 1866. Proposed what we call the Riemann hypothesis in 1859. Never been proven or disproven. Probably the most difficult challenge in mathematics."

He showed another slide.

"This is the mathematical expression of it. I don't expect you to understand it, obviously. Here's the thing. Most experts believe it's true. But if we could prove it, some people think the proof itself will involve the discovery of an algorithm that will lead to a new cryptology."

Willis stared at the unintelligible screen.

"Boil it down. What does it say?"

"It says a lot of things. The most interesting part of it has to do with the distribution of prime numbers. As you know, a prime number is any number that is divisible by itself and one, and no other number. The building blocks of all number theory. Like seven or thirteen or seventeen and so forth. We've proven that they're infinite. And there are fewer of them the higher up you go. Are they randomly distributed? A proof of the Riemann hypothesis would give the answer."

"Frankly, I don't know what the hell you're talking about," said Hawkin.

"Hawkin . . ."

Willis let the word hang for a second.

"You and I majored in the history of arts and letters. What was your senior thesis on?"

"Baldwin of Flanders."

"Right. It was quite good. But now Maynard gets his innings. All right, Maynard, what's the significance of all this?"

"Three things. First, there's some evidence that the Chinese have cracked it. They've started to send messages we can't decipher. Dalton will speak to that in a moment. Second, if we can prove it, the algorithms that result will open up their message traffic. But third, I get a bad feeling even hearing the Weber kid's name. We had a very bad time in Milwaukee—with him, and his whole tribe of idiot savants."

Gieck went to the next slide. It was a picture of Bernie Weber.

"A few years ago, we found out this kid could give you the prime factors of any large number in his head. He used to perform at math shows in Milwaukee as Mr. Pryme Knumber, the math rapper. When he was in high school. Remember? He and his brother, who called himself Dr. Kalen Darr?"

"I'd like to forget."

"We gave him a number to practice on, to see if he was legit," Gieck said. "We gave him the wrong number by accident. He caused us a hell of a lot of trouble."

"Except that he did write an algorithm we still use. It lets us read Chinese traffic again. Up until now. Maynard, tell us what's changed. And do it without giving Hawkin a headache. And me."

"Right. All cryptology up until now is based on trapdoor functions. We send messages in coded numbers that a computer can easily break. So, we multiply our coded message by a very large prime number that only we know. When we send it to our allies, they multiply it by their own very large prime number that only they know. They send it back to us. We divide out our prime number and send it back to them. They divide out their prime number, and they have the original message. Doesn't matter if an enemy intercepts it along the way. It would take a computer a thousand years to factor out our prime numbers."

"And that's what the Weber kid could do in his head."

"Right. But much more important, he showed how to do it in an algorithm. So now, as you know, we can read Chinese traffic, and they can't read ours. Or, I should say we could read theirs up until recently."

"So, what happened?"

"My turn."

Carroll Dalton took over the screen. He showed a picture of a Chinese general. "This is General Li Yu. Commanding officer of the Ministry of State Security, the Chinese intelligence agency. Until they went dark, we were picking up references to 'Riemann' and 'Praising Professor Yin Hou.'"

Dalton changed to a slide of a middle-aged Chinese man wearing a blue suit and glasses.

"This is Professor Yin Hou, a mathematician at Zhejiang University in Hangzhou. Some of our analysts who listened to the traffic think that Hou may have solved the Riemann hypothesis. If he did, most mathematicians think the proof itself would produce a new cryptology that we can't currently break."

"That's absolutely ridiculous!"

Gieck was angry.

"I met this idiot at a conference in New York. I saw him present. Forget the Riemann Hypothesis. He couldn't pass an undergraduate course in number theory. I think he's more of a political officer whom they plant in their universities to keep an eye on students."

"That's their method of espionage," said Willis. "Dalton, explain what they do."

"Right. They don't follow our model. They don't spend a long time developing sources or double agents. Instead, they send students and professors for short periods of time. They mostly steal IT, but some of them have gotten into our governmental agencies and defense contractors. Yin Hou recruits students for their Security Ministry to send them to the U.S. and Europe. I defer to Maynard on his competence as an academic."

"Bottom line," Gieck said, "they've changed their mathematical encryption methods for some communications, and we can't read them. They may have accomplished it by proving the Riemann Hypothesis. And it's a certainty that Yin Hou wasn't the one who proved it."

"So what should we do?"

Willis looked around the table.

"Gieck?"

"Personally, I don't think a college kid can solve this. I wouldn't waste much time on him. I'd work with our cooperating mathematicians and intensify that research. Increase the prize."

"Dalton?"

"Weber's just a kid. I doubt a kid could come close to doing what we need. I'd leave him alone."

"All right. I've heard enough"

Willis stood up and opened the door.

"Maynard, Dalton, you're excused. Thank you. Hawkin, please meet me in my office."

Chapter Eight

Lathrop Willis cut into a wedge of cheese on his desk and poured from a decanter into two Galway Crystal goblets. He placed them on a lacquered Japanese tray and walked over to Wayne Hawkin.

"I found an excellent sherry, Hawkin. And a five-year aged cheddar. Have some."

Hawkin took a piece of cheese. He took a glass and held it up. Willis held his in return.

"*Pocula elevate. Nunc est bibendum.*"

Hawkin nodded.

"*Bibemus.*"

"To your health, Z."

"To yours, Z."

They drank.

Both Willis and Hawkin had been members of Scroll and Key at Yale, a generation apart. Yale has nine secret societies whose student members, all seniors, tap their replacements from the incoming class. Scroll and Key, known as Keys, is the literary society. In fact, it's a principal recruiting ground for the CIA. Keys was founded in 1842, its structure made in jest to resemble a Papal Court. Its members are assigned names from mythology and literature. The leader is named Zanoni, Z for short.

Many familiar figures have been members of Keys: Cole Porter, Benjamin Spock, Gary Trudeau, Dean Acheson, Cyrus Vance, John Lindsay, a Mellon, a Rockefeller, and others. Like Willis and Hawkin, John Lindsay had been Zanoni. But Dean Acheson had been Volero, the court jester, and none of his professional accomplishments made up for the college slight.

"Hawkin, do you have the stomach for another go at the Webers in Wisconsin?"

"You know, I really don't. I found it damned unpleasant. No need for it. The kid can't possibly help us this time. I'd advise against ops. And Congress has stopped us anyway."

"The legislation simply says we can't do covert operations in the United States. It's unclear, though, exactly what a covert operation is."

"Willis, there are 150 pages of legislative history. I don't think it's unclear at all."

"I agree that they don't want us to go in and snatch people. Quite right. We'd only do that if I felt it was an emergency. But Hawkin, tell me this: is simply following someone a covert operation? I don't think so."

"Have you read the leg history?"

"Of course not. And no intention of doing it. I get the idea. We'll be reasonable."

"Willis, look. How about the obvious? The kid came around to helping us last time. You told me you called him then to thank him. Why not just call him? Meet with him. Ask for his results. Even put him on our payroll?"

"Can't do that. I personally think there's no way he can actually solve a problem like this. No one in Europe or the U.S. has solved it. And if I'm wrong, we'll find out what he comes up with anyway."

Willis slid a folder to Hawkin.

"And something else. You haven't seen this. From our sources on the ground. Read it. It wasn't the Chinese mathematician who solved the hypothesis. It was a Uighur boy, a teenager. They killed him and his parents. The Chinese are in Milwaukee now, following the Weber kid."

Hawkin was silent.

"What are you thinking of doing?" he said.

"We'll send two good men to Wisconsin. Young men. They'll trail the Weber kid. I'll tell them to find out if he's making progress on the problem. And who and how many are following him. If it's bad, we'll go in. If it's not, we'll get the FBI involved."

"Who are you sending?"

"Dustin Baker Eddy and Neville Scrimshaw."

"They were both Keys men, weren't they?"

"Of course. They're ours, Hawkin."

"I don't know them. Do they work together?"

"Better than that. They're a year apart. Eddy tapped Scrimshaw. And they were both at Portsmouth Priory together. Eddy was Scrimshaw's prefect in St. Benet's when Scrimshaw was a fifth former."

"They weren't Z, were they"

"No. Eddy was Thales. Scrimshaw was Chilo."

"Are they any good?"

"Plenty of promise. Smart boys. They'll let me know if they need backup."

"But no more rendition jets to Alabama. Like last time. Right"

"Right. Of course. Not for our side."

Chapter Nine

I was standing on the corner of 8th and Oklahoma, on Milwaukee's south side, with Bernie and Alderman Jimmy Fieblewicz. Fieblewicz used to be my alderman. Family friend. Up for reelection. Jimmy hired me for a grand a month to do his field operation, such as it is. Bernie and I were doing doors with Jimmy. Circulating his nomination papers.

Fieblewicz passed us each a map.

"We're doing a whole ward today. You guys'll come with for a couple blocks. Get the hang of it. Then we'll spread out."

We followed Jimmy up the walk to the first house, a tiny Lannon stone Mickelson. He knocked on the door. A man opened it.

"What do you want?"

"Mr. Ted Stimac?"

"What do you want?"

"I'm your Alderman. Jimmy Fieblewicz. I'm up for re-election, and I . . ."

"I know you guys. First thing you do is go and put all four feet and a snout in the trough."

"Not me."

"I'm onto you. You drive them fancy cars."

"That's a lie you heard. I got a '92 Park Avenue. Blue Book twenty-five hundred."

"Blue Book's higher'n that."

"No, it's not."

"It looks newer than that."

"I keep it clean. No rust."

"You wear them fancy clothes."

"It's a smear. I shop the sales."

"Heard you got real art in your house."

"That's a lie. Nothing but family pictures."

The man took the literature Jimmy handed him.

"Would you sign my nomination papers?"

"I'll think about it."

I took notes while we walked to the next house.

"Joe, there's two kinds of districts, ain'a?"

Jimmy pointed to the houses ahead of us.

"One, I go to the door. The lady answers. I see a cat in the corner. 'What a good-looking cat,' I say. She grins and holds him up. About a twenty pounder. He looks at me. 'This is Mr. Meow,' she says. 'Hi, Mr. Meow,' I say. I scratch his ears. I got a vote. Next time I'm there, 'How's Mr. Meow?' I say. She runs into the kitchen to get him. I scratch his ears. I got her."

"Okay," I said.

"I don't care what you see in the corner. You see an iguana in the corner. Or a dead body. Whatever. 'What a good-looking iguana,' you say. Or whatever. See?"

"Right."

"Then you got your Madagascar districts."

"Your what?"

"Fancy homes. I bust my ass for them. I go to their historic designation meetings. Get them tax credits for tuckpointing their goddamned houses, like they should do anyway. I'm at the doors. Lady answers. I ask for her vote. Lady looks at me like she swallowed rancid milk. 'I have a concern,' she says. 'I'm disappointed in your vote on the Madagascar resolution,' she goes. See, they wanted to name their capital as Milwaukee's sister city. But we already got twenty sister cities. I'm going, Madagascar. That's where they got them bald monkeys with the pointed ears and the big eyes, and that. We don't need that here. So, I vote present. But they sniff me out."

"You'll be okay."

"Gotta pay toll to the troll. Bernie, don't you do it when you get older. It's bad work."

"I won't," Bernie said.

"This ward's more your ear scratchers," Jimmy said. "We're okay here."

He knocked on the next door. A man opened it.

"I'm Slovakian," the man said.

"I'm very pro-Slovakian."

"That's all right then."

The man signed his papers and closed the door.

"Joe, here's the deal," said Jimmy as we walked to the next door. "Man opens the door and tells you he's a Yak. 'I'm very pro-Yak,' you say. See? Nothin' else."

"Got it."

At the end of the block, a Chinese man sat in a parked car, an old, pearl blue Lincoln LS. He listened to a speaker on his steering wheel while he watched the three figures at the other end.

"Joe, here's the deal. Man opens the door, and tells you he's a Yak . . ."

The Chinese man's phone rang.

"*Ni hou.*"

"Where are they now?"

"I'm watching them. It's quite strange. They are with an official. He goes to people in their homes and asks for help. The people insult him to his face."

"That is why their culture cannot survive. They have no respect for officials. Government cannot be left to the people. Have they discussed the problem?'

"There has been no discussion of mathematics. But the boy is doing directed study on the problem with a professor at the university. He is making progress."

"Continue to observe him."

"It will be so."

"*Bai bai.*"

"*Bai bai.*"

Jimmy Fieblewicz knocked on the next door. A pretty woman in her mid-seventies, blond with red lipstick, opened it. She was smoking a cigarette, holding the butt with her thumb and index finger from underneath, her wrist turned backward. She brought it up to her mouth and took a drag.

"So what do I got to do, Jimmy?" she said. "Strap a mattress to my back? You never come by."

"I come by. I need you, Tillie. I need your vote."

"There's a gentleman of the Chinese persuasion sitting in a car over there. Friend of yours?"

She pointed down the block. I turned but couldn't see anyone.

"Don't know him. Will you sign my papers, Tillie? Take a lawn sign?"

"You know I will, Jimmy."

She grabbed the clipboard.

"Drop it off."

Chapter Ten

Two men in their late twenties sat in front of Lathrop Willis' desk. One wore a blue blazer with red checked shirt and gray slacks. The other a Harris tweed jacket, corduroys, and a white shirt. The man in the blazer had thick hair that sloped over his forehead. His jaw was angular, his chin almost pointed. The other man had smooth, pink skin and a round face that made him look ten years younger than he was. They watched Willis finish a phone call. Neither spoke.

Willis hung up.

"So. Scrimshaw?"

"Scrimshaw, aye," said the man in the blazer.

"Were you in the navy, Scrimshaw?"

"No, Sir."

"Then let's avoid the 'ayes.' Eddy?"

"Sir."

"I want you both to do something for me. To take an assignment."

"Of course."

"It's an unusual venue. A population difficult to infiltrate. A strange culture. Uncooperative. A lot of nosy people, full of peasant cunning and resistive to instruction and bribery."

He pressed a button.

"I'll have Dalton in to brief you."

"Is it in Africa, Sir?"

"I'm afraid not. It's Milwaukee."

"You're joking. Of course."

"I am not. Briefly, it's this. There's a boy in Milwaukee with an extraordinary gift for mathematics. He solved a problem for us a few years ago that has proven quite valuable. But he made it difficult. We sent a man out there. Do you know Holz? Dieter Holz?"

"No."

"No."

"Good man. But they gave him a lot of trouble. Can't have that again."

Carroll Dalton walked in carrying several folders. He settled in an armchair next to Willis's desk. Willis lowered a screen on the wall and displayed a picture of a teenage boy.

"This is Bernie Weber. He's a person of interest to us. Nineteen years old, student at Milwaukee Community College. A few things you must know. First, he has deep mathematical ability. He may be on the verge of a breakthrough we need to know. And second, the Chinese know about him. They're in Wisconsin now, and they may approach him. Conceivably he could be in danger, although that's not certain."

Willis opened the next picture.

"Here's his uncle. Joe Weber. Surrogate father to the boy. Protects him. The boy's father is in a mental hospital. You can expect the uncle to be crafty and persistent. Has friends in the Milwaukee Police Department. Be very careful with him."

Willis changed to a picture of another man with thin hair, Lennon glasses, and an extraordinarily thick black beard.

"This is Terry "Shit Theory" Norris. Friend of the boy's father. Did all but a dissertation in mathematics. Owns a small roofing company. Very small. He's the only employee. Has helped the boy and his uncle in the past. Be careful with him, too."

"How did he get his name?"

"He supposedly proved that if you have a mediocre hand in seven-card stud, Hi-Lo, like two low pair and a ten-nine low, you're better off going both ways than just picking one."

He changed pictures. An attractive woman in her twenties with long dark hair appeared.

"Joe Weber's girlfriend, Frannie Ferraro. Spanish lecturer at Milwaukee Community College. Caused us a lot of trouble in the past."

Willis changed pictures a final time to a man in his thirties in a police uniform. "This is a Milwaukee police officer. Jerry Piano. He's protected the kid in the past. Will interfere with us, but also the Chinese. Strong in the police union. Can involve other officers when he has to. Dalton, explain what we're after."

"Okay."

Dalton handed each man a folder.

"Here are your instructions. Where you'll stay. All Milwaukee landmarks and history of the city. All public officials. Background on the Weber kid. On his family and friends. All of their contact info. Pictures and bios. Everywhere you're liable to find them. We believe he's made important progress in solving a very difficult mathematical puzzle, called the Riemann Hypothesis. If he has, we need his work."

"And the Chinese know about him, may be after him? Tell us more about that," Eddy said.

"Right. The Chinese use a different intelligence model than we do. They use students and faculty from China who pretend to come here to study and work. In fact, they come here to steal. IT. Research. They go into industry or academia. It can be hard to anticipate. Their identities aren't concealed."

Willis interrupted him.

"The point is, we know they're familiar with the Weber kid and his work. We know they're following him. What we don't know is what they'll do if he gets close to solving the hypothesis. I don't think they'll hurt him. Or take him. But I'm not sure."

"So we'll protect him?"

"Not exactly."

Willis sipped from a glass of port. He didn't offer a glass to the others.

"Congress has forbidden us to conduct domestic ops. Obviously, if you found an imminent danger to a U.S. citizen, we'd alert the FBI and cooperate with them. But here's what I want you to do. I want you to monitor his work at all times. His computers. His family's home. His carrel in the library where he's doing some of his research. I want his work on mathematics, *any mathematics*, sent back to us immediately. I want you to follow the Chinese who are monitoring him. Locate and identify them. And if there's even a hint of a threat to him, we need to know that immediately."

"Will do," Eddy said.

"That's all, gentlemen."

Willis's phone rang.

"Hello?"

"Willis. This is Hawkin. Have you talked to them?"

"Just finished. They'll be in Milwaukee tomorrow."

"Okay. Somebody's knocking. I'll call you later."

Hawkin hung up.

"Come in."

Audrey Knapp walked in and closed the door behind her. She was dressed in a knee-length, seafoam green shirtwaist dress, with a stand-up collar and a belted, cinched waist. Her thick hair was pulled back and held with a tortoise-shell butterfly clip. She wore black shoes with kitten heels and ankle straps.

She sat in the chair in front of Hawkin's desk.

"Have you been looking at the traffic? The chatter?"

"Of course," Hawkin said.

"I'm worried. They have men in Wisconsin already, following the boy. They think he's getting close to finding a solution to the problem."

"Right. But we just sent two men ourselves. They'll keep an eye on things."

"Who?"

"Neville Scrimshaw and Dustin Baker Eddy."

"Goddamn it, Wayne! You're sending in the Pink Panther? And who, the Pink Squirrel? That's ridiculous. They're newbies. They have no math skills and no experience. The boy's in serious danger! We picked up Chinese chatter about sending a plane from Vancouver if he won't take the bait. What do you think that's all about?"

"Not certain. If we see more, we'll alert the FBI."

"The FBI is doing the domestic threat from the Middle East. And from Chechnya and Bosnia. And drugs. How many of them are they supposed to infiltrate? They can't do the Chinese. They don't have the manpower. Or the expertise."

"We have to stand down. Congress clamped down when they found out about our domestic surveillance. If we do it again, it'll have to be damned important."

"It *is* damned important!"

"What do you want me to do?"

"Send me out there!"

"I seem to remember you've had combat training?"

"Seem to remember? I was at the academy, ready to go into the field. The agency asked me to go NSA because of my math background. I can handle myself."

Hawkin walked over to the window. He looked out with his back to Knapp.

"Audrey, I can't do that."

He didn't turn to face her.

"I can't send you. But I can do this. You have three months leave at full pay and benefits. To prepare a plan for me on better coordination with municipal police forces on domestic terrorism. I don't care where you do your research. Your report can be verbal."

"Wayne. Thank you!"

He still didn't turn around.

"But also this. If something goes wrong in your 'research,' I can't help you. And there will be no agency communication on your assignment. No internal record. No chatter. No nothing. If you need anything, call me directly. And only me."

"Understood. And thanks."

"And one other thing, Audrey. If you do see Eddy and Scrimshaw, don't let them get in your way."

Chapter Eleven

Dustin Baker Eddy and Neville Scrimshaw walked into Karl Ratzsch's, a German restaurant on Mason Street in Milwaukee. The exterior showed an Alpine mountain scene, with wooden slats neatly spaced across the plaster wall.

"I Googled the menu, Eddy. Outstanding rations. It's the oldest German restaurant in Milwaukee."

A stout man dressed in lederhosen with a shock of blond hair over his forehead greeted them at the door.

"Two?"

"Yes."

He escorted them to a table next to a stained glass window, which showed the medieval German trickster Till Eulenspiegel riding on a donkey, holding an owl and a mirror. More than a hundred ornate beer steins rested on shelves and railings throughout the restaurant.

A quartet of four musicians, two men and two women well into their seventies, was performing in the corner. The men, dressed in lederhosen, played accordions. One wore an alpine hat with a red feather. The women in dirndls were singing an aria from *Die Fledermaus.*

A Chinese man stood outside the restaurant talking on his phone.

"They have gone inside."

"Are they meeting someone?"

"I do not know."

"Enter and watch them."

"Yes."

He hung up and stepped inside.

The man who had seated them handed Eddy and Scrimshaw two menus.

"I will return."

"This is great stuff, Eddy. You don't see it everywhere. Food you can sink your teeth into."

They studied the menu. Eddy pointed to one of the pages.

"The wine list can inflict pain, but it can also show mercy. Scrimshaw, there are actually wines here for less than fifty dollars."

They both chuckled.

"*Bruderlein. Bruderlein und Schwesterlein . . .*" sang the two women.

The blond man in the lederhosen returned with a pad.

"I will be your waiter. The waitress called in ill. I am also the maitre'd. My name is Bosco Wallenfang."

They nodded.

"The name itself is Swedish. But my mother was a Hohenlohe."

"Are there any specials?"

"The soup. Wolf peach and basil."

"Wolf peach?"

"Tomato."

"Okay."

Eddy studied the menu.

"I'll have the wolf-peach soup. Sauerbraten with red cabbage and potato pancakes. And strudel for dessert."

"To drink?"

"A kir."

Wallenfang wrote in his pad.

"Do you know what a kir is?" said Eddy.

"Yes. So does the bartender."

"He appreciates the restraint necessary to make a great kir?"

"Who?"

"The bartender."

"What?"

"To impose an ever so pale layer of creme de cassis, a slight blush on the excellent Bourgogne Aligote? It should be layered like a Georgia O'Keeffe painting, with pale shades of lavender on pale shades of gold."

"I'll tell him."

"Man lebt bei mir recht fein."

"I'll have the same," Scrimshaw said.

Wallenfang nodded and walked away. The man in the Alpine hat walked up to their table, his accordion still strapped to his chest.

"I am Fred. We take requests."

"Do you know the Whiffenpoof song?"

"No. But for you, we will play 'Auld Lang Syne.' "

Fred walked over to the Chinese man.

"I am Fred. We take requests."

The death stare.

"For you we will play musician's choice."

Fred returned to the corner. They started playing "Auld Lang Syne."

Dustin Baker Eddy buttered a warm pretzel roll.

"This is a slice, this town. Pushover. Never been here before. You?"

"Never."

The Chinese man's phone vibrated. He slipped into the empty bar.

"Wei."

"The boy's made advances. Where is he now?"

"With the uncle. He's never alone. What has he done?"

"We looked at his laptop . . . hold on."

General Li Yu turned to Professor Yin Hou. The professor nervously crossed and re-crossed his legs as he sat in a chair facing the general's desk.

"How serious is it?" the general said.

"The utmost. The boy has replicated the advances on the problem that were made only after the mathematician Siegel deciphered Riemann's notes in 1932. Those notes had been disjointed and unreadable. Because of Siegel, we realized that Riemann himself had solved much of the problem."

"So?"

"Several things. The notes were incomplete. But the boy has duplicated the work deciphered in Riemann's notes. And we know that he did it independently. He reached some conclusions that aren't in the notes."

The general picked up his phone.

"Can you hear me?

"Yes."

"There is now urgency. We will extend the scholarship offer to the boy. He may decline. If so, we will activate the Vancouver option. But do not execute until I tell you."

"Yes, General."

"And the two men in the restaurant?"

"Yes."

"Neutralize them. Do it without scandal to us. Simply make them ineffective."

"It will be so. I request permission to employ the Trump option."

They both chuckled.

"Granted. But leave no footprints."

"I will be a cat walking on velvet. *Zai jian*."

The man in the bar went back to his table. Bosco Wallenfang put down a tray next to Scrimshaw and Eddy's table.

"Two wolf peach."

His phone rang as he set a bowl of steaming tomato soup in front of Scrimshaw.

"Excuse me."

Wallenfang answered it.

"What? Okay. What time will you be home? Okay."

He hung up and placed a bowl of soup in front of Eddy.

"I apologize. It was my son, Florian. Tonight, he is attending a *verdorbene fleisch partei.*"

"A what?"

"A spoiled-flesh party. Some of the guests will be over thirty."

He picked up his tray.

"I will be back with the sauerbraten."

Chapter Twelve

A woman rang the upper doorbell at a duplex on North Booth Street in Milwaukee's Riverwest neighborhood. This is the bohemian quarter separating the mansions on the east side bordering Lake Michigan from the inner city to the west. Holton Street, the western border of Riverwest, is referred to in Milwaukee as the Mason-Dixon line.

A woman in her twenties with long, dark hair and grey-green eyes answered the door.

"Yes?"

"My name is Janet Bachman. Would you be Frannie Ferraro?"

"Yes. How did you know? What do you want?"

"I'm a reporter with the *New York Post*. I'm on book leave from the paper. I'm doing research in Milwaukee. Could I come in?"

Ferraro looked out to the street and up and down the block. No one else was in sight.

"Do you have identification?"

"Of course."

The woman handed her a New York State driver's license and a business card with the *New York Post* logo, and, underneath, "Janet Bachman, Reporter" with a general number, direct line, fax number, and private email address.

"Come in."

Ferraro seated the woman on a sofa in the tiny living room and took the armchair across from her.

"What can I do for you?"

"The *Post* is trying to change—not change exactly—but *expand* our image. Right now, we're seen by some as a tabloid. Headlines with bad puns about sex scandals. You know, Weiner and Spitzer and that sort of thing. Lots of pictures about the mob and various murders."

"And?"

"I'm on leave to write a book. It may appear as a serial story. More serious than we normally do. My topic is the state of math and science in our colleges. Seventy percent of our electrical engineering degrees go to foreigners. Almost that many in math and physics. We want to sound the alarm."

"So, what do you want with me?"

"We're covering math competitions around the country. You're Bernie Weber's aunt?"

"Not yet, actually. I'm his uncle's fiancée. Joe Weber. We live together. He's out right now."

"Good. Anyway, we know that Bernie Weber recently won a national math competition in Madison. Our editors love the story. Domestic math genius. I'd like to spend some time with you and interview him about his work for my story."

"Excuse me please. Just a minute."

Frannie Ferraro went upstairs to her bedroom and closed the door. As she picked up the phone, she pulled the woman's card from her pocket and dialed.

"Hello?"

"Hello. I'm calling from Milwaukee. I'd like to speak with Janet Bachman, please."

"Just a minute."

The call transferred. A voice mail kicked in.

"This is Janet Bachman. I will be on leave from the *Post* until the Tuesday after Labor Day. Please dial zero for assistance."

It was the same voice as the woman downstairs.

Ferraro dialed zero.

"Can I help you?"

It was a woman's voice, no-nonsense and abrupt.

"Can I speak with Janet Bachman?"

"Sorry. She's on leave. Book leave."

"Is she out of town researching a book about math?"

"Honey! I don't know where she is. Am I her mother? She's doing a book. I think in Milwaukee. That's all I know."

"Thanks."

Ferraro returned to the living room.

"So, Janet, what exactly are you asking me?"

"I'd like to set up an interview with Bernie. Look at where he does his work. What are his hobbies? Sports? Shadow him a little to do a day-in-the-life of piece."

"That might be all right. I'll talk to Bernie and Joe. I'll call your cell."

"That'd be great. Thank you."

The woman got up to leave.

"I'll look forward to hearing from you, Frannie!"

She adjusted the tortoise-shell butterfly clip in her hair as she walked outside.

Chapter Thirteen

General Li Yu stood at attention. A man behind a large desk was speaking on the phone. He was in his sixties, pudgy, with plastic-framed glasses. He wore a suit with a red tie, and his hair was lightly oiled, combed straight back and perfectly in place.

"*Bai bai.*"

The man hung up and rose to extend his hand to the general.

"Welcome."

Li Yu bowed.

"Thank you. It is an honor to be with you, Yan Shifan."

The leader waved him toward two chairs.

"Join me over here. Would you like some tea?"

"If I may join you."

Yan Shifan poured two teas and handed one to the general.

"To the success of Violet Light."

Li Yu raised his in turn.

"To its success."

They drank.

"But General, I am concerned."

"May I help in some way?"

"You may. We are an ancient civilization, five thousand years old. The greatest the world has ever seen. The rest are barbarians. The success of Violet Light will determine the future of China, and mark its greatness for another thousand years."

"And it cannot fail."

"Unless the Americans find out its real use. If they do, they will destroy it. The isolationist element in their country will be set back. The Americans are too powerful to be stopped if they summon the will. We must have time to make Violet Light fully operational so that it is beyond attack."

"And it will be so."

Yan Shifan sipped again from his cup.

"It will be so if it remains secret. I am concerned about our cryptography. What is the status of the American attack on the hypothesis?"

"Trivial and unsuccessful. The Riemann Hypothesis is the most difficult problem in all of mathematics. They cannot break our codes."

"They cannot break our codes unless they solve it. What do I hear about a boy in Wisconsin?"

"Beneath the dignity of your attention. Son of a peasant family. Some facility with numbers. Did some tricks at a math competition. A charlatan. If all of the mathematicians in the world can't do it, it's irrational to think that the boy can."

"The Uighur boy did it, General."

"Yes. And he had an accident. Professor Yin Hou is the man who solved it."

Yan Shifan smiled.

"An idiot. I knew him at University. An incompetent, a sycophant."

He stopped smiling.

"And unreliable. We have discovered that he has boasted of having solved something important. The Americans may discover what happened and gain access to the solution through conventional espionage."

"What would you like me to do?"

"Two things. Professor Hou must be removed. He is a danger to the State."

"Perhaps a trial? For treason?"

"I don't care how you do it. Commence with a human flesh search."

"And the other thing?"

"The American. The boy in Wisconsin."

Yan Shifan's voice hardened. His eyes showed anger.

"He is a brain-poisoned youth, blind to right and wrong. Such a person must be stopped. Forever."

General Li Yu bowed.

"It will be so. Forever."

Chapter Fourteen

Frannie came into the living room and threw her arms around my neck.

"Joe, isn't this exciting! For Bernie!"

Bernie sat in an armchair across from me. I could tell he was pretty pleased with his bad self. He tried not to grin as his eyes darted around the room.

We were playing Shafskopf. Sheepshead. The Sheeps. Me, Terry Norris, and Jerry Piano. Terry's a roofer, a classmate of my brother Jimmy when they were in the math PhD program. Jerry's a cop.

We were playing three-handed, the skill game, two in the blind, quarter a point. Not four-handed with four in the blind, where everybody goes in and tries to get trump in the blind. And definitely not five-handed, where somebody picks you as a partner and drags you down.

"Let me see the letter again."

Jerry picked up the envelope. It was addressed to Bernie at his dorm. The return address had no street or P.O. Box. There was no postage stamp. It just said, People's Republic of China, ZHONGGUO, with a red flag underneath. The flag had five gold stars in the upper left-hand corner and one large star and four smaller ones in a semi-circle to the right.

"Pretty neat."

Jerry pulled out the letter. The letterhead had the same words and red flag as the return address box.

"Dear Mr. Weber," he read. "Congratulations on your victory in the American mathematics competition this spring at the University of Wisconsin. We wish to advise you that you have won the Lei Feng Prize in Mathematics for young mathematicians under the age of twenty-five.

You are the first American to win the prize. It pays your tuition at a university and graduate school of your choice for up to seven years."

Frannie smiled as Jerry continued.

"The prize will be awarded in Beijing on September fifteenth. We will defray the travel expenses for you and one companion. Please contact Professor Chu Jih-Nien, Wuhan University, Wuhan, Hubei Province, P.R. China 430072."

"That is terrific!"

Frannie gave Bernie a hug.

"I'll go with, Bernie," Terry said. "You need somebody who knows some math."

"Me," Jerry said. "I'll go. You need security over there. Lot of crazies running around. You got your commies, your terrorists—the whole goddamned shmear."

The doorbell rang. Frannie answered it.

"Janet! Come in."

She brought her into the room. Janet was a good-looking woman, about thirty-five, with thick hair pulled back in a tortoise shell clip. She was carrying a briefcase.

"Guys, I want you to meet Janet Bachman. Joe, I told you about her. Janet, I'd like you to meet my fiancé, Joe Weber. And Terry Norris, our friend I told you about, the roofer. ABD in math. And Jerry Piano, our friend, the police officer. And Bernie, our math genius!"

Janet smiled at us all and gave a little wave.

"Guys, Janet is a reporter for the *New York Post*! She's on leave writing a book on math and science in colleges. She's going to follow Bernie for a while 'cause he won the contest. Bernie, you'll be in a book! And I told her about the Chinese prize you won!"

We all basked in Bernie's new fame. Pretty damned good. Pretty good for a bunch of guys playing the Sheeps on Booth Street in Riverwest.

"But you know, Janet had something interesting to say when I told her about the Chinese prize. She said there'd been problems with it in the past. It might not be what it seems. Bernie should be careful about going. Janet, could you tell the guys what you think?"

"Sure."

Janet pulled a laptop from her briefcase.

"Let me see the letter."

She inspected the letterhead and the return address.

"It's a fake."

She opened her laptop.

"We've done a lot of research on China and their math instruction and their prizes. In the past, the Lei Feng Prize was a gimmick their intelligence agencies used to get foreigners to China, basically to steal their discoveries. In some cases, they died."

A video appeared on her screen in Chinese, with English subtitles. The caption said, "Learn from Lei Feng Day."

"Lei Feng was a soldier in the Chinese army in 1952," Janet whispered as the video played. "He was hit on the head by a falling telephone pole and died. They made him into an icon."

"Lei Feng said, 'My only ambition is to be a rustless screw for the great cause of revolution,' " a narrator explained in Chinese, according to the translation.

A picture of a young man in a cloth cap and quilted jacket appeared on the screen, followed by soldiers marching.

"Lei Feng collected three hundred pounds of cow dung during one day in the Chinese New Year to help the farmers," said the narrator.

The screen changed to a picture of Feng in bed, reading by flashlight. The caption said, "Lei Feng reads the collected works of Chairman Mao."

The flashlight was off, and the room was fully illuminated.

"And here is the rope his mother used to hang herself when she was attacked by a greedy landlord."

Janet clicked on another link.

"The national myths under the communists are fake. Look at this."

Another video appeared.

"Learn from these heroes of the revolution," the subtitle said, while a narrator spoke rapidly in Chinese.

"Iron Man Wang, who dog-paddled in a vat of cement when there was no machine to mix it for the workers."

A picture of a fat man swimming in what looked like a tub of oatmeal appeared on the screen.

"Shi Chuanxiang, the night-soil collector, who worked tirelessly to help the farmers."

A picture appeared of a guy in a padded cloth jacket holding a shovel and appearing to sneak up behind a cow.

"And Wang Yiqing, the electronics worker who assembled five million radio parts without a single mistake."

She closed the laptop.

"Boy, you sure know a lot about China," Frannie said.

"It's a big part of my book. Here's the thing. The people in China are fine. But the government is corrupt and brutal. We found out that the last person who won a Lei Feng award died in a plane accident under unusual circumstances. The plane landed safely, but he wasn't on it."

"No way," Terry said.

Jerry jumped in.

"I tell you what. I'll go with Bernie. They wouldn't pull that shit on an American."

"You think so?"

Janet grew animated.

"They have a zoo over there that ran out of animals. So, they put a dog in the bear cage, a chow, and pretended he was a bear. They put a German shepherd in the wolf cage, and said he was a wolf. This is fake, too. Anything they do is fake. Bernie, I'd strongly advise you to hold off on this."

"But it's free tuition. And a trip to China."

I was skeptical.

"What are they going to do—bump him off? A kid from Wisconsin they never heard of?"

"Frankly, yes. Maybe. Bernie'll get a full ride at any grad school in the country. He has a full ride now. Not many people can do what he does. He can go to China in a few years on a student exchange. I think this invitation is a fake."

"We'll think about it," I said. "Hard to give up a free trip to China. Hey, Bernie? What are they going to do—steal Bernie's action? He doesn't have any."

"I just wanted to let you know what our research shows," Janet said. "What are you guys playing?"

"Schafskopf. Want to play?"

"Sure. What are the rules?"

"Kind of like bridge. But trump is always queens, jacks, and diamonds, in that order. I'll deal out a few hands to show you."

"Sounds interesting. Deal me in."

Chapter Fifteen

Neville Scrimshaw and Dustin Baker Eddy approached the door of Karl Ratzsch's for another dinner. They heard a voice singing in the alley "ABC, *die Katze lieb im Schnee. On the farm every Friday, it's rabbit-pie day! Run, rabbit, run! Run, rabbit, run!*"

They looked around the corner and saw Bosco Wallenfang sitting on a packing crate, gently stroking the fur of a magnificent white rabbit. The rabbit sat contentedly in his lap, blinking, while Bosco Wallenfang scratched behind its ears. The rabbit's cage sat on the ground by his side.

Bosco looked up at them.

"I am on break. You will be seated by Gottlieb. I will be inside shortly."

He looked back at the rabbit.

"This is my little Hasenpfeffer," he crooned. "But there is no hasenpfeffer on the menu. No! My little Hasenpfeffer's profession is to win blue ribbons at the state fair. 'Here is my bunny, with ears so funny.' I will protect . . . my Hasenpfeffer."

As Scrimshaw and Eddy entered the restaurant, a thin man in lederhosen picked up two menus. He wore a large button that showed a man in a leather jerkin, holding a crossbow, walking with a young boy through a mountain meadow. Underneath, it said, "When human rights met depredation, God made the Swiss Confederation—1291."

"I am Gottlieb Zgraggen. Follow me please."

He escorted them to a table near a quartet that was playing arias from *Cosi Fan Tutti*.

A gorgeous woman in her late twenties sitting at the bar stared at them as they entered. She took out her phone as they were seated.

"Hello?"

"Where are you?"

"At the restaurant. You were correct. They are here. And they are staying at the Hyatt."

"Deploy. And do not fail."

She put her phone back in her place and signaled a waiter.

"Table for one. That one over there."

She pointed to a two-top next to Scrimshaw and Eddy.

"That one has to be cleared. Would you like to be seated elsewhere?"

"No. That one. And order me a salad. Have it waiting. I must leave soon."

"All right. It will be just a moment."

A man wearing a green, collarless jacket and an Austrian hat with a large crown and narrow brim sat on the next stool.

"Have you been to Austria?" he said in a heavy accent.

"No."

She looked away.

"In Austria, I hunt the deer and the foxes and the hares. But I do not hunt the brown bears. We do not like them in Austria. They are immigrants from Slovakia and Slovenia."

Another strange one. Where's my table?

"But the European Union makes us have fifty of them."

She didn't respond.

"They were shot. I am only telling you the truth. There were two left."

A waiter walked over to her.

"Your table is ready."

"My brother, Odo, is calling me from Linz last week," the man said. "Bruno has been shot. There is now only one brown bear in Austria."

"Don't follow me!" she said, and walked to her table.

Scrimshaw and Eddy ordered two kirs. They observed the beer steins on every ledge and the lederhosen and dirndls of the musicians.

Scrimshaw pointed.

"Definitely a slice, Eddy. But all this German stuff gives me the shivers. Reminds me of the course on Kant."

"I dropped it."

"I should have. I couldn't understand the first two pages. Some people say he's just a bad writer. I think he did it on purpose to look profound. I don't think he's that big a deal, actually."

"So what happened?"

"I told the prof, Westerfield. I said, 'You know how you can make this intelligible? You know the joke about German students having to read Kant in translation? Well, have it translated into Finnish. Then, from Finnish into Basque, without looking at the original. Then, from Basque to Japanese, Japanese to Aztec, and Aztec into English, all without looking at the original. Any ideas he actually had will sit there like shiny little nuggets.' "

"What did Westerfield say?"

"Basically, he screwed me. I barely passed. You know what I think?"

"What?"

"This food is great, but it's bad for clear writing. It causes indigestion in weak stomachs. Kant wrote so badly because of indigestion."

"Did you tell Westerfield that, too?"

Scrimshaw didn't answer. He kept looking at the beautiful woman sitting at the next table, facing him. She occasionally dabbed at her eyes while she ate her meal. When she noticed him looking, she slowly crossed her legs.

"*Abbondanza!*" Scrimshaw said. "I'll be glad when we get back to D.C. I spent the day in the Weber kid's neighborhood. Not a damn thing going on. No sign of anything out of the ordinary."

"Right. I followed the kid all morning. His uncle picked him up. I followed them to the uncle's house. I'll pick it up tomorrow."

"Right."

Zgraggen came with their drinks.

"Order, gentlemen?"

"I've got to go with the Wiener schnitzel. Eddy, look at this. With an egg on it! You can get it with an egg on it!"

"It is the Viennese custom," Zgraggen said.

"Excellent. I'll take it. With the spaetzle and the red cabbage. Eddy?"

"The same."

"Very good."

Gottlieb left with the menus.

Scrimshaw stood up.

"Excuse me."

He left to go to the rest room.

As Scrimshaw walked back to the table, the woman looked up at him briefly. She attempted a shy smile, holding his eye slightly longer than the norm. Her blouse was unnecessarily unfastened to the third button.

He sat down and sipped his kir.

"You know, Eddy, that's a damned good-looking woman. I think . . ."

A large busboy with pink, baby skin and hair sticking out like the bristles on a cheap brush started to clear dishes from the table just behind them. His large pale blue eyes stared with disturbing intensity around the room.

"Groggy! Groggy!" he chanted softly as Gottlieb Zgraggen walked by.

Zgraggen was not pleased.

"Show them your holiday photo, Bert," he said, as he headed for the kitchen.

Bert scurried over to Eddy with an insolent grin on his face.

"Do you want to see it?"

"No."

"Thank you!"

Bert reached for his pocket. He looked like a demented giant.

"Look!"

He pulled out a picture of himself standing at attention, wearing a headdress and a goat mask. Behind him stood an Indian dressed like a goatherder, holding a whip made of parrot feathers.

"Mardi Gras! Every year I go!"

"Enough," Eddy said. "Neat town. A real slice. But I've really had enough. I . . ."

The leader of the quartet, Fred, interrupted him before he could finish.

"Ladies and gentlemen, we will do now something a little different. It has been given to me from God, the gift of being able to dance and play at the same time. I will now demonstrate."

The quartet started to play "The Hokey Pokey."

"You put your left foot in; you take your left foot out . . ."

Fred wiggled his left foot in front of him as he played the accordion.

Scrimshaw looked at the woman once more. She recrossed her legs. Her napkin fell on the floor, and she leaned down slowly to retrieve it.

Fred interrupted them again.

"You put your backside in and shake it all about."

A couple sitting closest to the quartet flinched as they watched Fred wiggling his leathery ass twelve inches from their rice pudding as he played, bent over the entire time.

"Marvelous stuff, Eddy. Very native. Deliciously cheap. I do get tired of Mory's, you know."

The woman got up to leave. She stopped at their table and put her hand lightly on Scrimshaw's arm.

"I recommend the bratwurst, gentlemen. They are exceptionally . . . firm."

She looked back at Scrimshaw as she left the restaurant.

"Damn it, Eddy. Why the hell do I have to be on assignment?"

They finished their meal and headed back to the hotel. As they passed through the lobby, Scrimshaw noticed the woman from the restaurant sitting alone in the corner of the lobby bar near the piano.

The elevator stopped at the tenth floor first and Eddy got off.

"Breakfast tomorrow?" he said. "Seven?"

"Seven. See you tomorrow."

The elevator went up to fourteen, and the door opened. Scrimshaw started to get off, hesitated, and stepped back inside. The door closed, and the elevator descended to the first floor. He returned to the lobby.

The woman still sat alone, looking out the window. Scrimshaw sat at the bar and ordered a cognac.

"May I join you?"

He looked up. The woman stood next to him, holding her drink. Her cheeks were streaked with tears. She tried to smile at him.

"Of course."

He stood up.

"Please, join me."

She sat down.

"I noticed you at the restaurant."

"And I noticed you."

"What is your name?"

"George. What is yours?"

"Cindy."

"That's a nice name. Are you okay?"

She hesitated.

"Yes."

She started to cry softly.

"What is it? Can I help?"

"Oh, George. I've been abandoned."

"Can I help you?"

She didn't respond immediately. Finally, she dried her cheeks.

"My boyfriend left me. He was an older gentleman. Very generous. Now I am alone."

She gently touched the back of Scrimshaw's hand.

"I am so afraid. Would you escort me to my room, George?"

"Sure. Now?"

"Yes. Please."

Scrimshaw put a twenty-dollar bill on the table and they headed to the elevator. Several couples stepped inside with them. She held his arm and their bodies touched. She briefly put her hand on his and then slowly withdrew it.

She turned to him at the door to her room.

"Would you come in for a moment? I don't want to be alone."

Scrimshaw followed her inside to a softly lit room.

"Thank you, George."

She put her arms around his neck to kiss him.He gently ran his hand across her skirt and started to unbutton her blouse. She opened her mouth slightly to take his tongue. Scrimshaw closed his eyes. He didn't notice the dim, red light pulsing on and off in the corner.

Chapter Sixteen

Yan Shifan sat back on a sofa in his office with his foot in the lap of a girl who was giving him a pedicure. His bathrobe was slightly open at the chest. General Li Yu sat stiffly facing him.

"So, you've heard what the idiot has done now?"

Yan Shifan scowled. General Yu didn't respond. He kept looking at the girl and back to the leader.

"Have you done what I told you?"

Again, the general looked at the girl.

"All right. We will speak alone. You may apply the lacquer."

The girl painted his toes with Ballet Slippers, an almost-but-not-quite clear polish with an ever-so-faint hint of pink.

"You may leave. The general wants to speak in private."

The girl bowed. She gathered her equipment and scurried out.

"Professor Yin Hou. You heard he did it again?"

"Some of it," said the general. "Tell me."

"Like a rat hiding in the curtains, the furry pest awaits his chance," Yan Shifan recited. "Flushed with wine and insolence, he again told some students he had made a great discovery that protects our secrets. And for the first time, he mentioned Violet Light. If the Americans find out, they will destroy it. That cannot happen."

"The Americans know about Jade Rabbit. Our vehicle on the moon. It's been in the press."

"But they do not suspect what comes next. They do not know about Violet Light. And they won't until it's deployed."

Yan Shifan pressed a remote. A door opened on the wall to reveal a large TV. He pressed again. A chart of names and dates appeared.

"I remind you that we are the oldest civilization on Earth. Five thousand years old. The Han nation. Once the most powerful. We must be so again."

General Yu read the dynasties on the chart. Xia, Shang, Zhou, Qin, Han, Jin, Sui, Tang, Liao, Song, Jin, Yuan, Ming, Qing. He skipped among the emperors. Zhong Ding. Wai Ren. Jian Jia. Zu Yi . . .

"The Americans once owned space," Yan Shifan said. "They had complete power and then they gave it up. They lost their national will. We have put Jade Rabbit on the moon. India and Iran are ready to follow. But they must not discover Violet Light."

"I fully agree."

"I repeat my order. Professor Yin Hou must be removed. He is too stupid to do his job. Too indiscreet. We needed him to take credit for solving the hypothesis if necessary. But he continues to make errors even when it is explained to him by competent mathematicians. And his tongue moves when liquor or girls are present. The mere mention of Violet Light can result in the Americans' discovering it. And destroying it."

"The case against him is in process."

"The means are up to you. But Professor Yin Hou must be neutralized. Forever. And I want it done quickly."

"It will be so."

General Li Yu bowed to Yan Shifan. He picked up his hat and left the room.

Chapter Seventeen

Neville Scrimshaw and Dustin Baker Eddy sat in front of Lathrop Willis's desk as he spoke on the phone. Wayne Hawkin sat in an armchair on the side. Willis didn't pay the slightest attention to anyone.

"Yes, I'm calling for Lamar. The Congressman. Is he in?"

"Yes. Just a moment. Who's calling please?"

"Lathrop Willis."

"One moment please."

A man's voice appeared from the phone.

"Willis! Good to hear from you. What's up?"

"I need you to do something, Lamar. I'm calling you as the head of the House Intelligence Committee. What's this I hear about a Chinese mathematician being invited to a confidential briefing at the NASA space center in Houston? A Professor Yin Hou. Are you crazy over there?"

"Lathrop, relax. There are political realities. The Speaker wants to reach out to them. He thinks that Asians are the only minority we can get, and we're on defense. The Democrats have a lock on 40 percent of the vote in this country, and it's growing. They'll pander to anyone. I'm not saying I like it, but it's a fact."

"They come to steal, Lamar. They just put a vehicle on the moon. Jade Rabbit. Technology stolen from us. They stole most of the technology they're using to fight us. Why not just Skype the goddamned briefing into the cafes in Beijing while you're at it?"

"Is there a special security issue in this briefing?"

"Hell, yes. And you know what it is."

There was a long pause.

"You still there, Lamar? You hang up on me?"

"I'm still here. Do I have your assurance there is a special security issue with this briefing?"

"Damned right. Can you get some Republicans on your side?"

"I will. I'll talk with the Speaker. He's good on this. He'll let me get it done. Then he'll say it's a shame if they attack him on it, but he did what he could, and I beat him."

"Can you get some Dems?"

"Yep. Congressman from Louisville. Good man, with a head on his shoulders. He'll round up his posse. When we each need to get around our flakes to get it done, he and I can do it."

"Thanks, Lamar."

"Always call."

Willis hung up. He glared at Scrimshaw and Eddy. They sat staring at the floor.

"You've heard of photoshopping, Scrimshaw? Studied it in training, didn't you? Let me show you a bad example."

A video appeared on a wall screen. It showed Scrimshaw leaning back, eyes closed, wearing a red baseball cap that said "CIA." A sign on the wall behind him said, "CIA Interrogation Center." The woman kneeling before Scrimshaw wore a hijab.

"Outstanding work, Scrimshaw! First rate! You idiot! What were you doing out there? You were on assignment! I didn't send you to a Vassar mixer."

Scrimshaw and Eddy stared at the floor. Willis looked back at the screen.

"This video was sent to every government in Asia, Africa and the Middle East. The Chinese did it. I must say they're getting better at photo shopping. But still amateurs."

Willis pointed to the screen.

"See how your fingers look as if they're slipping through the cloth in her hijab? And the baseball cap looks like it's welded to your head over there. B-plus job. In the old days, they'd have seven-foot-tall party officials standing next to a two-foot peasant. Or two people standing a foot off the ground."

"Yes, Sir."

"This has set us back. Badly. Got the Fuzzy-Wuzzies all lathered up."

A video of a burning building appeared on the screen.

"They burned a Coptic church in Cairo," Willis said.

A picture of a clergyman with a full beard appeared.

"A Greek Orthodox priest kidnapped in Eastern Turkey. Look at the beard on the rascal, Hawkin. Magnificent. Guinness material. Hope he's okay."

Videos of angry mobs running through cities came next.

"Four Shiites killed in Baghdad. Five Sunnis in Syria."

Willis turned off the screen.

"Pakistan demanded one hundred million dollars to stay in line. That's more than they charge when we drone a wedding. The insiders steal half, and the other half goes to tribal chieftains to keep their socio-paths in line. We don't get much bang out of it."

"I'm sorry, Sir. I . . ."

"That's irrelevant. You did it. You're compromised. You are too, Eddy. Neither one of you is to return to Milwaukee. We were damned lucky to keep this out of the press."

"Will it ever appear?"

"No. We convinced *The New York Times* that it's a fake. The pho-toshopping did it for them. But I think the real reason is their mindset. They found it impossible to believe that we'd be interested in Milwau-kee."

"What can I do, Sir? I love the agency. I want to stay here."

Willis stood up and walked to the window. A light drizzle made the grass look exceptionally green.

"You are Chilo. Son of Arbaces. A Keys man. We need our men in the agency."

"Thank you, Sir!"

"Don't thank me so soon. You are compromised. You will return to training and to an analyst assignment. We'll determine in the future whether you can be safely reintroduced into the field."

He turned to face them.

"Eddy, I assign no blame to you. But we have to assess the depth of the damage. You will be assigned to analysis until we determine where we can redeploy you safely. Now, you may leave. I have to speak with Hawkin."

Willis and Hawkin waited until they'd left.

"There's something that bothers me, Hawkin."

"What's that?"

"We picked up chatter. Professor Yin Hou used a new term we hadn't heard before. 'Violet Light.' They don't coin terms lightly. It's a project. We must find out what it is."

"We have our people over there on it, don't we?"

"Right. But they can't find anything. Must be deeply encrypted. And I'm worried about our Project Sif."

"Can you give me more information?"

"Yes."

The screen on the wall lighted again. Willis pressed a button.

"Project Thor," the screen said. Underneath it, "Kinetic Bombardment."

"A variety of treaties forbid the deployment of weapons of mass destruction in outer space," said Willis. "SALT II, the Anti-ballistic

Missile Treaty, the Outer Space Treaty. Our government has decided to abide by them because of our superiority over China in existing weapons systems. Of course, the Chinese cheat. We have privately told them that if they violate the treaties and deploy nuclear weapons in space, we will take that as an attack on the United States and will respond immediately. We will destroy their satellites and might retaliate further. So far, they haven't tried it."

"Good."

"But we know they will cheat. No treaty bars any of us from deploying conventional weapons in space. So, we are developing a weapon that is technically conventional but will deter them from attacking us for the foreseeable future."

"Is that Thor?"

"Not quite. The idea behind Project Thor was first suggested at Boeing in the 1950s. The idea is to deploy orbiting tungsten poles with fins and a guidance system. They look like telephone poles. Twenty feet long, a foot in diameter, satellite controlled, with an impact speed of Mach 10. They're technically not weapons of mass destruction. But if you deploy enough of them to rain down on the enemy's cities, they'd have the same effect."

"Don't our ICBMs do the same thing?"

"Yes and no. Thors get to their target in half the time of an ICBM. They're much more difficult to detect on radar and defend against."

"Don't the Chinese know the concept?"

"Of course. But until now, it was mostly science fiction. That's the reason for Project Sif. In Norse mythology, Sif was the wife of Thor."

"What does that do?"

"The two main practical obstacles to Thor are that its destructive capability is small, about eleven tons of TNT, not much more than our conventional bombs. And atmospheric heat would melt non-tungsten parts on the weapon."

"What does Sif do?"

"We've solved the two problems. We can increase the kinetic energy by a factor of ten. And we've developed a tungsten shield that will protect the guidance system. Sif is the completed project ready for deployment."

"What are you worried about then?"

"Congress. You know, Hawkin, we effectively have no government. The Republicans would shut down the government, cut all funding, and stand by and see the Chinese rise to first place. They'd rather run deficits and have the Chinese buy our paper than do the responsible thing and fund the government we need."

He poured two glasses of sherry and handed one to Hawkin.

"*Pocula elevate. Nunc est bibendum.*"

"*Bibemus*," said Hawkin.

"The Democrats would let everyone in the world walk into our country," Willis said. "There are billions of people in the world who kill each other over religion, ethnicity, caste, and appearance; and they all brutalize their women. Then, they come here and bitch about discrimination. We're losing the collective will to unassailable power. And we're facing the Chinese, those brutal bastards. They're more race conscious than any nation."

"Is funding for Sif in danger?"

"In danger? It won't happen unless we create the right kind of pressure. Effectively, *we* are the government when it comes to defending the United States, Hawkin. You and me. And the Keys men now and in the future, who will run this agency."

They sipped their sherry in silence.

"You know, Willis, I'm worried about the Weber boy in Milwaukee. Why would the Chinese go to the trouble to take out our men there? What are they planning?"

"Who knows? Get the FBI involved. I've got too much on my plate right now. The boy's irrelevant. Can't imagine the FBI couldn't handle it."

"Okay. See you."

Hawkin returned to his office and picked up the phone.

"Audrey. It's Wayne. They compromised our men. Had to pull them. You're on your own in Milwaukee."

"I know. I heard."

"Any activity?"

"Yes. They sent the boy a fake invitation to come to China to give him an award. I tried to dissuade them, but I'm not sure I can."

"I've tried to get the FBI involved. They're stretched too thin. They'll only respond to an immediate threat. Be careful out there. You're next if they find out about you. Don't hesitate to use force if you deem it necessary."

"I won't. Wayne, there's one thing I need. Can you send in body snatchers? If I have to take stronger measures, we can't leave them on the ground for the police to find."

"We don't have many teams. Haven't used them domestically before."

"I know. I'll try to stay non-lethal. But I'd have to get them out of here. And there might be value in interrogating them."

"Look. Audrey. I can't risk it. I have men embedded in every mosque in New York and New Jersey. And in Florida. We shouldn't be doing that, of course. And now you want me to risk all of that for ops in Milwaukee we also shouldn't be doing?"

"Wayne, the Chinese threat is long term. It's economic. And demographic. The military threat to us is in the Pacific"

"So, what if they do take the kid? Which I doubt. For what? He can't break this problem. No one has so far."

"Except one of theirs."

"And one of ours will, too. But not a kid in Milwaukee who wore fake green ears in math circuses in high school."

"Wayne. Please. I'm staying out here. And I need it."

Hawkin paused.

"All right. I'll send in a team. The ones I pulled from Milan. They were discovered after their last grab. I'll embed them at the Milwaukee airport as mechanics. They'll have a plane. The code to activate them will be on your private website. When you do, they'll go to your phone."

"How much time do they need to respond?"

"From notice to arrival, maybe half an hour."

"When will they arrive in Milwaukee?"

"Within forty-eight hours."

"All right.

"And protect yourself first, Audrey."

"Will do."

Chapter Eighteen

General Li Yu sat behind his desk, reading a newspaper. His secretary intruded.

"A telephone call, Sir. It is the leader."

The general folded the paper and picked up the phone.

"The removal of the two men in Milwaukee? It was successful?"

"Completely successful. It was shown to the problem governments in Asia and Africa that they had raped a Muslim wife and mother. They were exposed. We gained at the expense of the Americans. And the two men were withdrawn from Milwaukee."

"How was it done?"

"White teeth sing, and a slender waist dances."

"Most satisfactory. You will now move in to take the boy."

"We will. But there is still an obstacle."

"An obstacle?"

"Yes. Another agent, a woman, is embedded with the family. We listen to the conversations in the house. She pretends to be a reporter."

"Remove the whore. Leave no evidence."

"We will."

"And Professor Yin Hou? He is removed as I ordered?"

The general paused.

"Not as yet. The human flesh search begins tomorrow. It will give context to his trial for treason."

"I am getting impatient. We must cut the weeds and pull up the roots. It is not enough to cut the stems. I do not want to have to call again."

"I apologize. It will be done with the utmost speed."

"*Bai bai.*"

"*Bai bai.*"

Chapter Nineteen

Janet Bachman drove us to Terry Norris's house in Riverwest. Bernie sat in the back seat. I rode shotgun. It was noon on a nice sunny day.

"So what's the plan today, Joe?" Janet said.

"We're going by Terry's to pick him up. Then, we hook up with Jimmy Fieblewicz and do some doors."

"How do you know Norris?"

Bernie jumped in.

"He was in a math PhD before he dropped out. Same class as my father. He was Dad's best friend."

"How's your Dad doing?"

"Good. They got him on better meds."

We parked in front of a house on Weil street. Terry was waiting. As he brought us into the living room, we introduced Janet.

The phone rang in a car parked at the corner. A Chinese man answered.

"*Wei.*"

"Where are you?"

"In a car. Parked near the house of Terry Norris. The boy just went inside with his uncle and the agent. The woman."

"You are monitoring their conversation?"

"Yes. Through the uncle's phone."

"Two things. Report back immediately about any discussion of the problem."

"Yes."

"And the woman. Neutralize her. Today. They have not accepted the invitation to Beijing. She is the cause."

"I will."

"I said today."

"I understand. I will obey."

"*Bai bai*."

The phone went dead.

"So, Bernie," Terry said. "What you got now? Somebody chasing you on a math thing again?"

"Not really. At the competition, they gave me a math problem that's kind of neat. A hypothesis. I'm trying to prove it."

"You told me. The Riemann Hypothesis?"

"Right."

"That's a ball buster. Don't know much about it. We had it in one course. Me and your dad. What do you want to know?"

"So, in your grad course, did you do anything on the partition function?"

"Sure."

"So, the formula that shows the partition for each number? Did anyone ever prove a pattern in how they increase for each number? Like the partition for eight is twenty-two. And the partition for nine is thirty. And the partition for ten is forty-three. Do you think the increases are random?"

"No clue. Didn't get into a proof."

"You know," Janet said, "you might be onto something, Bernie. There is a formula to show the partition number for all numbers, but no formula to show the distribution of primes. And yet the partition-function proof spun off a technique called the circle method that's used to show what numbers can be written as the sum of three prime numbers."

"How'd you know that?" I said.

"Picked it up in my reporting. General knowledge. And one more funny thing, Bernie. For the circle-method proof to work, you have to assume that the Riemann Hypothesis is true."

The Chinese man in the car dialed.

"*Wei.*"

"They are discussing the proof for partition numbers. And then the relation between the circle-method and the hypothesis. The same insight that Professor Yin Hou arrived at."

"You are mistaken. Professor Yin Hou did not discover it. He is guilty of treachery. He has brought together undesirable forces and formed a faction as the boss of a factional group. Workers and students throughout the country have broken into angry shouts that a stern judgment should be meted out to the anti-party, counterrevolutionary factional elements."

"I am sorry. I had not heard."

"I am surprised you had not heard."

"I apologize. I will be more knowledgeable in the future."

"Very well."

"Then, if I may ask. Who did discover it?"

"That will be announced as needed."

"I understand."

"But the matter is now more urgent. The insight of the youth could lead to the discovery. We will send more agents. And it is essential that the woman be eliminated."

The phone went dead.

We headed south to Water Street, and then onto South Kinnickinic until we got to the Colectivo coffee shop.

Alderman Fieblewicz was sitting at a table next to a thin woman with a mane of gray hair swept up and held by a clip. She wore a black polyester pantsuit, blue pinstriped blouse, and black sneakers. She peered at us through tortoiseshell glasses as we sat down.

"Hey, guys. I'd like you to meet Trixie LaFond, my campaign manager. She's starting today."

I'd heard of LaFond. A Milwaukee institution in every election cycle. Did races for aldermen, supervisors, and judges. Knew everyone. Everyone liked her. She'd get the basics done. And she wasn't expensive.

"I'll lay out the challenge. And then how we win." Trixie said. "The challenge is, the election is four months from now. If Jimmy wins, he looks solid. Maybe a shot at mayor next time. If he loses, he's just another starving old cat out in the alley, looking for food."

Fieblewicz took offense.

"Wait a minute once!"

"Bite me rightly. You know it's true. Jimmy, if you aren't in office, you don't exist. Here's your biggest problem. And here's how you beat it."

She swigged her coffee.

"The problem is, the district is fifty-five percent Latino now. Crept up on you. Santiago Flores is running again. If they all vote, you lose. But their turnout is lower than anybody else. So, you've got a chance. Thing is, you got to turn out damned-near all the Anglo vote. So, you triangulate."

"What's that?"

"Slick Willie pulled it off. Clinton. You take an issue from the other side and run with it. Willie ran with death penalty and no more welfare. Flogged them. He was hard-core Dem on everything else. He confused everyone enough to slip in. You're gonna do the same."

"Death penalty and the welfare. That ain't going anywhere now."

"Not them. You're going to go nuclear on the phonics."

"The what?"

"The phonics."

"What's that?"

"A way of teaching kids. You do away with spelling, word order, grammar, normal stuff. They just hear sounds."

"Who cares?"

"Jimmy."

Trixie was being patient.

"No one cares. It's a fake. But you need damned-near every vote to turn out. You've got lots of lefty Dems in your district. But also a decent number of tea-bagger wingnuts. They might stay home. Except that the phonics is a wing-nut issue, so they're confused. It's the law in Teabaggia. They're thinking, is Jimmy winking at me? Is he showing me love? Does he get it? Could Jimmy go commando for us on everything later? So they turn out. They'll never vote for Flores. But now they aren't staying home."

"All right. Fill me in later on. Let's do doors!"

Trixie handed us ward maps, divided into sections.

"I'll go with Bernie," Janet said.

"Okay. You do section one. Terry Norris? You go with them."

"Right."

"Joe, you go with Jimmy. Section two. I'll do three by myself. Meet back here at five p.m."

Trixie handed us three sacks of lit. Simple cards, with a picture of Jimmy looking into the camera smiling, and "Jobs, health care and lower taxes" printed underneath. On the back was a Packer schedule.

We hit the doors.

A driver in a car at the end of the block watched people come out of Colectivo carrying three sacks. He dialed.

"Yes?"

"The boy is with the agent. She may be armed."

"Follow them, but do not interfere now. We are not ready to take him. But the woman?"

"Yes?"

"Tonight, after she leaves them. Follow her and neutralize her."

"I will. They are strange people."

"In what way."

"Their conversation in the coffee shop. The worker, a woman, insults the candidate to his face. Says he is a starving cat in the alley."

"What?"

"And their whole plan is to trick the workers in a clumsy fashion with false promises."

"The flatulence of a dying culture. Proceed as ordered."

We had a couple of blocks under our belt when we walked up to a bungalow with neatly trimmed bushes.

"Joe, here's the deal," Jimmy said. "After this one, you take the next one. See what it's like."

"Okay."

Jimmy knocked. A thin, somber woman in a bathrobe opened the door.

"Susie!"

He grinned.

"And how's my little Rusty? Meow!"

"G-gone!" she cried. "Rusty d-died!"

Her eyes were moist.

Fieblewicz went instantly sorrowful.

"That's terrible! Dearest Rusty! I shall miss him so."

She went colder than a well digger's ass.

"Rusty was a girl," she said quietly.

She had him. A torpedo right in the engine room.

"I misspoke! I'm so sorry. Dear, dear Rusty."

Damn! What am I, a vet?"

She stayed stone cold. Milked it. She silently took a piece of lit and closed the door without saying a word.

"Your turn next, Joe."

Jimmy handed me the ward list. He looked glad to take a break.

I rang the bell on a small ranch. I looked at the sheet when a man answered. He was built solid, mid-fifties, with a crewcut.

"Mr. Elfskin Growlbutt?"

"What? Who the hell are you! It's pronounced 'Grallbeaut!'"

He glared at me.

"But Elfskin?"

The man looked at his feet.

"Pa was big on his Shakespeare."

He looked up at me.

"It's Bud to you!"

He was furious.

"What do you want?"

"This is my friend, Jimmy Fieblewicz. He's up for reelection. I wonder if you'd take some lit . . ."

"Don't want none of that!"

He slammed the door.

Jimmy was patient with me.

"Joe. You don't just walk up to a guy's door and call him names. It ain't nice."

"But it was his name."

"So what? He didn't give it to himself. Some guys don't like their name."

Jimmy shrugged.

"Joe. Look. You go up to a door. Say there's a problem with the name. You go 'am I speaking to the gentleman of the house?' See? He grins. See? It's beautiful. He's a gentleman. He likes you. They vote for guys they like."

We knocked off at five to head back to Colectivo. The others were already there.

"So, here's the deal."

Trixie had a calendar spread out on the table.

"From now on, there's gonna be some discipline in this campaign. Jimmy does money calls from eleven to two. Doors from two to five."

"Every day?"

"Every day. Evenings are for events. Here's the schedule."

She pushed another calendar to Jimmy.

"I lined up the big one!"

Trixie was pretty damned pleased with herself.

"What's that?" I said.

"Jimmy's speaking at LAUC! Just before the election."

"What's that?"

"The Latin American Unity Conference. It's the umbrella organization of all Latino groups from Milwaukee and statewide. I got some buddies there. They're gonna let Jimmy speak!"

"Is that a good idea?" I said. "I mean, doesn't Flores have that locked up?"

"Not really. Flores will be there with his posse. But a lot of people don't like him. And we win either way. We'll get press there. The story is, Jimmy goes into the lion's den and such. If he gets a good reaction, it's a story. And if Flores stacks it, Jimmy has backup talking points. Triangulates. Lobs some grenades. Food fight. Great squeeze! We can't lose."

"Okay. I don't know."

"I need wine."

Trixie slumped back in her chair.

"Janet, you want to come?"

"Sure. Where we going?"

"Winners. Club on Marshall. See you there at eight?"

"Sure. I'll drop these guys off and meet you there."

"Eight twenty north Marshall."

"Got it. At eight."

As they left Colectivo, the Chinese man in the car a block away dialed.

"*Wei.*"

"They have left the coffee shop. The woman is going to a bar."

"This is your opportunity. How will you do it?"

"Perhaps in the bar. Perhaps follow her to her car."

"Do not fail."

"I cannot fail. She is a woman, unprotected, by herself."

"*Bai bai.*"

Chapter Twenty

The sign over the door said "Winners" in red and yellow neon letters. The club was already starting to fill up.

A cluster of swordsmen and hard luck cases stood at the bar. Their unblinking eyes swept the room, looking for signs of drunkenness. Several locked in on Janet as she walked past them to a table by the window where Trixie was sitting.

"Over here, Girl."

Trixie pushed a bottle of wine toward Janet as she sat down.

"Hope you like the Pinot."

"Absolutely."

Janet poured herself a glass and raised it.

"To Jimmy's victory."

"To Jimmy."

They drank.

"You think it's easy in this business? Putting up with the guys? You think I don't know what they call me behind my back? 'The She-Wolf of Door to Door'? Jerks."

Trixie drained her glass and poured another.

"You're a good-looking gal. You have a boyfriend?"

"I was in a relationship. It didn't work out."

"So, what's your racket? What do you do?"

"I'm a reporter. Working on a book about the state of math and science in America today."

"So, what are you doing here?"

"Bernie Weber won the national math competition. Joe's letting me follow him as a feature for my book."

"Oh. Right. Jimmy filled me in."

"Bernie? Is he going to spend a lot of time on the campaign with Joe, or what?"

"Hope so. We need bodies. Truth is, volunteers aren't crawling out of the woodwork."

Through the window Janet saw a Chinese man approach the front door. It was starting to get dark.

"Excuse me while I go to the powder room," Janet said.

When she walked to the ladies' room, Janet saw the man standing in the hallway in front of the men's room. As he started toward her, she ducked into the bathroom. A girl was standing in front of the mirror, adjusting her red dress. She was in her early twenties, with plenty of makeup, and black roots showing through her blond hair.

Janet punched some numbers into her phone, then a text:

How soon?

A text came back:

Twenty minutes.

The girl at the mirror smoothed her dress.

"Kinda slutty, isn't it?" she said, admiring herself in the mirror. "Didn't have the balls to wear it before."

"Honey, can you help me?" Janet said. "There's a guy after me. Out in the hallway."

"What?"

"I had a restraining order out on him. He's not real dangerous, but kinda creepy. I don't want to talk with him. Could you walk me to my table?"

"Any time, Girl. We ain't putting up with that."

Janet hooked her arm through the girl's, and they walked out into the hallway. The Chinese man started to take a step and then froze in place.

"Beat it!" said the girl in the red dress as they walked by him out into the bar.

"Thanks, Honey."

"Any time!"

Janet hit her forehead lightly when she rejoined Trixie. She put a twenty-dollar bill on the table.

"Trixie! I forgot! The computer guy is coming over to fix my PC tonight. I'm having trouble using it. I think it's a virus."

"No problem. Don't worry about me."

"I'm so sorry! It took me two weeks to get this appointment. My treat next time."

"Good."

The hallway to the front door was empty. Janet hesitated at the bar. She sat down next to a heavy young man in jeans and a navy sport jacket. He could barely sit up on the barstool as he swigged from a glass of bourbon. He looked at her, looked away, then looked at her again.

Janet leaned toward him and let her fingers linger on his arm.

"I bet you have a serious rep for badassery."

He threw back his shoulders.

"Kinda," he slurred.

"You play football in college? I bet you did."

"Yeah."

"What'd you play?"

"Line. I mean, backfield."

"Awesome."

"What's your name?"

"Lavinia."

"I'm Roger."

"Awesome. You know, I hate to head home alone. Could you walk me to my car?"

"Every day!"

Roger leaped up, and almost fell. Janet rose to slip her arm in his and steadied him as they walked toward the door.

The Chinese man was standing on the sidewalk half a block away, pretending to read a map. There was no one else in sight.

Janet pointed in the other direction.

"I'm that way."

She almost had to hold Roger up as they stumbled to the corner. She turned him up the quiet side street. The Chinese man hurried to catch up.

Janet reached gently into her purse. As he got near them, she spun Roger around and fired around his back. The man went down convulsing. She tased him again.

Roger raised his hands and stood very still.

"I'm sorry! I didn't mean to touch you! Or whatever!"

"Stand still."

She knelt down, pulled out a small syringe, and jabbed the man in the arm. Roger stood motionless as she rose.

"Oh, Roger. You're so sweet! It isn't you. Help me make him more comfortable."

Janet grabbed him by one arm. She motioned Roger to take the other. They dragged the man up across the grass and put him behind a bush. He lay there unconscious.

Roger started to back up.

"I'll be going."

"It's my landlord, Roger. You know how they treat a single girl who can't pay the rent."

"Your landlord! Of course!"

Roger gave out a nervous laugh.

"You're a good guy, Roger. Stay with me 'til I get in my car."

"Uh, I better not."

He started to back up.

"I need you, Roger. Now!"

Janet took his arm.

A white truck with a sign that said "Prime Movers" drove by them and pulled over. Roger stood still. Two men in jeans got out.

"Behind the bush," said Janet.

They picked the man up and put him in the back of the truck.

"Who's that?" Roger said as they drove away.

"The landlord-retrieval service. You know."

"Of course. That's what I thought."

His eyes darted back and forth, looking for an escape.

"I need you to do one more thing for me, Roger. Stand here for five minutes. Perfectly still. You understand?"

"Of course. Of course."

"Thanks, Roger."

Janet walked to the corner and disappeared. Roger stood, looking up and down the empty block. Finally, he got the courage to stumble back to Winners with the ultimate "You ain't gonna believe this."

Chapter Twenty-One

"Chang Sheng is missing."

General Li Yu looked around the table for a reaction. The other officers said nothing.

"He followed the woman to the bar. We have heard nothing since. His tracking implant has been removed."

"The leader will be displeased," a colonel said. "But the human flesh search for Yin Hou has had an effect. He is in hiding. We have located him. If he does not commit suicide soon, we will arrest him."

"Good. Here is our plan. We will reveal the identity of the woman to the boy's uncle. They will reject her. The honey trap will then approach the family friend, Terry Norris. She will seduce him. She will agree to move in with him. When she has gained the confidence of the family, she will guide our men to the boy. They will bring him to Beijing."

"What if she is unsuccessful? Will it not cause suspicion?"

The general chuckled.

"She has already been successful in removing the two agents. Consider these pictures."

He pressed a button, and a picture of a woman appeared on a monitor. She was gorgeous, in her late twenties, with long, dark hair. She stood on a beach in a leopard-skin bikini, kissing a bullfrog cupped in her hands.

"This is the woman. And this is Norris," the general said.

A picture appeared of a slightly balding man, about forty, with a bushy beard and closely set eyes. He was slender, with a weak chin.

They all chuckled.

"He is a half-starved pervert, blind to reason," said the general. "Not skilled at causing a flutter in a maiden's heart."

They all laughed.

"They dress their dogs in human clothing. But they do not impress us," the general said.

"His jade chowrie handle is not of prodigious size," said a colonel, to more laughter.

"It is inconceivable that this woman will be unsuccessful with a lonely man approaching middle age. She will seduce him easily. Failure is impossible."

The men nodded.

"But how will we get the boy out of Milwaukee?"

"Our plane will come from Vancouver to pick him up. There is little inspection of private aircraft in America. They will file a flight plan back to Vancouver but change course over Canada and return to Beijing."

"The Canadian authorities will not object?"

The general laughed.

"How? A private aircraft radios near Vancouver and announces that they have decided to return to China. What can they do? Shoot it down over the Pacific?"

"I understand, General. But the woman? Their agent? She may remain to cause trouble."

"We will eliminate her."

The men nodded again.

Chapter Twenty-Two

"Wayne!"

"Where are you, Audrey?"

"Still in Milwaukee. I had to neutralize one of them."

"I heard. I spoke with the team. We'll be interrogating him shortly. Good work."

"The point is, they're on to me."

"Right. Be careful. Change hotels."

"I have."

"What is the boy's progress?"

"Surprisingly good. They must know it, too. I expect more activity."

"Do whatever you need to do to protect yourself."

"I will. If they come in numbers, I'll need more men."

"They're yours. Just tell me."

"Okay. Goodbye."

She put the phone in her pocket and rang the bell. Frannie answered the door.

"Janet. Come on in. They're all ready."

Frannie and Janet walked into the living room. I was sitting there with Bernie and Terry.

"Okay, guys," I said. "We're set. Trixie and Jimmy are meeting us at the Azteca on Oklahoma. We're doing the Jackson Park area."

My phone rang. It was on the table. Frannie answered it.

"It's for you, Joe. A woman."

I took the phone.

"Yes."

"Are you Mr. Joe Weber?"

"Yes."

"This is Janet Bachman. I'm a reporter with the *New York Post*. I'm returning your call."

I damned near fell on the floor. I looked at the woman on the couch.

"Let me take this inside," I said.

I walked into the next room.

"Who are you?"

"My name is Janet Bachman. I'm a reporter. You called me?"

My head started to hurt.

"Where are you?"

"In Arizona."

"Tell you what. Give me a number to call you back. Your cell and your office."

"Okay."

She gave me two numbers. I hung up and took Janet Bachman's card out of my wallet. I dialed the number on the card.

"Hello. *New York Post*."

"Janet Bachman, please."

"She's not here. Out on book leave."

"Where is she? Do you have her number?"

"I think Milwaukee. Can't give out private numbers. Want to leave a message?"

"No. That's okay."

I hung up and dialed the office number the woman had just given me.

"*New York Post*."

"Janet Bachman. please."

"She's not here. She's on leave for a few months. Book leave."

"Did she leave a number?"

"Sure."

The woman gave me a number, which matched the cell.

"Thank you."

I dialed the cell.

"Hello?"

"Ms. Bachman? This is Joe Weber. What can I do for you?"

"I got a message that you called me. Had a tip?"

"What are you writing?"

"A book on drugs. How they get to the New York market."

"How long have you been at the *Post*?"

"Fifteen years."

"Thanks. I think there's been a mistake. I don't have a tip for you."

"Okay. Sorry."

I called New York information.

"The number for the *New York Post*, please."

"Stand by."

The number matched what the woman had just given me.My heart pounded. I started to get a little pain in my chest. I walked back into the living room.

"Janet. Could I see you in the kitchen?"

She walked in with me.

"Get the hell out of here!"

"What are you talking about?"

"You're not Janet Bachman."

She was silent.

"Who the hell are you?"

She didn't say anything.

"This is more undercover chasing Bernie around! I'm tired of this NSA shit! I told them last time, *no more*! Get out of here!"

Frannie heard me raise my voice. She came running into the kitchen. The woman walked slowly out the front door.

Chapter Twenty-Three

Wayne Hawkin's phone rang.

"Hello?"

"It's Audrey. There's been a development. The Chinese outed me. Joe Weber just told me to get out. He knows."

"Are you coming home?"

"Wayne, I can't. The boy's in danger. What does the FBI say?"

"Too busy. They don't see the threat. What about the Milwaukee police?"

"They don't have the expertise. There's a family friend who's a cop, but Joe will tell him about me."

"What do you want to do?"

"Stay here. Change tactics."

Hawkin was silent.

"Wayne?"

"I can't approve that."

"Wayne!"

"But you still haven't prepared your plan. How you do that is up to you."

"Wayne, thank you! And the team at the airport is still in place?"

"Still in place."

"I owe you."

"Be careful."

Chapter Twenty-Four

Terry Norris saw a woman crying at a bus stop as he walked home in Riverwest. She was pretty, in her twenties, with thick, black hair. She was dressed in a short, blue jean skirt and a white blouse.

"Are you okay? Can I help you?" Terry said.

"I don't know who to talk to," she said, rubbing the tears from her cheeks. "My boyfriend just left me!"

"Can I do something?"

"What's your name?"

"Terry. Terry Norris."

"I'm Cindy. Sit down with me, Terry. Please."

Norris sat next to her. She took his hand.

"Terry? Can I tell you something?"

"Sure! Yes."

She started to cry again.

I'm so afraid of being alone. Is there somewhere we can go?"

He was quivering.

"Yes! Uh, the Poet's Corner. Yes! The Poet's Corner."

"What's that?"

"A bar. A really nice one."

"But you have to be gentle with me, Terry. I get drunk very easily."

"Okay! Okay! I will."

The Poet's Corner was half full when they arrived. Several ropes hung from beams on the ceiling down among the tables. A balding man with a full beard and no moustache came to take their order.

"Cash in advance or tab?"

"Tab," Norris told him.

After the man took their order, he pulled down on the nearest rope. A wicker basket descended to the floor. Terry Norris took off one of his shoes and handed it to the man. The waiter put the shoe in the basket and pulled it back up.

"Terry. What is this?"

"Oh. You can pay when you get each drink. Or you can run a tab and pay at the end."

"So?"

"Some guys run out before they pay the tab. So, you give up one of your shoes. They see a guy with one shoe walking out, they chase him."

Oh, my God, I don't know if I can take this. I will not put up with strange. That I will not do. I've worked Europe and Asia. But I don't do strange.

"Isn't that interesting!" she said.

There was an awkward silence. Norris was desperate to break it.

"My buddy from high school? He was on TV. He's the head of reptiles at the zoo. Someone got bitten."

"I pray it didn't bite him on his private parts," she purred, extending a leg.

"Yeah. Wow! That'd hurt! I hope not."

You idiot! What do I have to do?

"Wine for the lady. And the beer for you."

The waiter placed a glass of Pinot Grigio in front of Cindy and a Miller Lite near Terry.

She adjusted an earring.

"I feel naked without my jewelry," she whispered.

Norris' hand trembled as he picked up his glass.

Cindy's phone rang.

"Hello?"

"Cindy? It's Jill. Got a question about price?"

Norris could hear her. Cindy covered the receiver.

"Business call," she said to Norris. "Won't be long."

She uncovered the receiver and turned her back to him.

"Yeah, go ahead."

She listened.

"He'll only pay a hundred. A hundey? You kidding me?"

She listened some more.

"For that, he only gets a Trump helicopter."

Norris leaned over the table, pretended to adjust the saltshaker, and tried to catch snatches of the conversation.

"What is it?"

Cindy lowered her voice even more.

"You know what it is. What? Right. That's it."

Cindy drained her glass.

"Terry, tell you what. Let's go somewhere a little more private. Do you live alone?"

"Yes. Yes I do."

"Good. Let's go there. We can play a game."

"What kind of game?"

"I'll teach you. Get your shoe back."

It was a short walk to Weil Street. A replica of the Remington cowboy on a rearing horse filled the coffee table in front of the sofa. The wallpaper was Green Bay Packer logo footballs.

Norris turned on a lamp next to the sofa. He stood awkwardly without saying a word. The woman sat on the sofa. She parted her legs briefly as she sat down. Terry quickly looked away.

"Sit down next to me, Terry."

He obeyed.

"You have a deck of cards? What can we play two-handed?"

"We can play two handed Schafskopf. Sheepshead. It's hardly excellent, hey."

You gotta be kidding me!

"Okay. How do you play it?"

"We each get five cards down and five cards up. And six each in our hands. When you play an up card, you got to turn the down card up. We take tricks and count points. Trump is always queens, jacks, and diamonds, in that order. Rank of queens and jacks is clubs, spades, hearts, diamonds, in that order."

"Interesting."

I've got a bad feeling about this. Should've sent one of my girls.

"Oh. And two other things. We only use the sevens and above, and tens are higher than kings."

"You have any alcohol, Terry? A girl gets thirsty."

"Beer?"

"Bring me one."

Terry returned with two cans of Miller Lite and a deck of cards. Cindy swigged from the can while he stripped the deck. He dealt the first hand.

She put her hand on his wrist.

"We have to make a bet, Terry."

"What kind of bet?"

"A big bet."

Do I have to do all the work?

"We could chug a beer if we lose."

"I know, Terry! We'll play for clothing."

Terry was getting aroused. He squeezed his legs together.

"Okay! Okay!"

He started to deal. Suddenly Cindy began to cry.

"Are you okay?"

"Yes."

She sniffled and put her hand on his leg.

"Oh, Terry, sometimes I feel like such a slut."

Terry squeezed his legs tighter.

"I think you're very pretty, Cindy," he said shyly.

She tried to smile.

"Do you want a suggestion?" he said.

"What?"

"Maybe you could develop some cat-like wiles? I think they help women."

She exploded in laughter.

"That's a damned strange thing to tell a woman!"

Her laughter faded to a sniffle.

"You don't think I have any, do you?"

She started to cry again.

"Any what?"

"Caaatliiikewillles!"

She dragged it out through her sniffling.

"I'm sorry! Forget I said it."

Cindy stretched back on the sofa, knees together, ankles apart, as Terry picked up his cards. She contemplated him without pleasure as she permitted her knees to part slightly.

Thin hair, bald on top, heavy glasses, slight frame, slobbering like a starving mongrel. But life is imperfect. You never knew.

Cindy sat up to pick up her cards. Terry played the eight of clubs from his up cards. Cindy pounced with an ace from her hand.

"Didn't think I had it? Did you?"

The hand went quickly. Terry lost by eight points. Cindy tugged on his sleeve.

"Off with the shirt."

He tossed his shirt on the sofa next to her. He dealt quickly.

"Terry! You snarfed up all the queens."

She struggled with her hand. When they counted points, she hadn't even made schnitz, a quarter of the points.

"You're supposed to lose double when you don't make schnitz," he said.

He started to lose courage.

"I mean technically."

She stood up slowly. Terry went pale. She lifted one leg slowly to remove a shoe. Then the other. She tossed both shoes onto the rug.

"My turn," she said as she sat down. "You're losing the undershirt, Terry. It's coming off."

The next string of hands went badly for Terry, depending on how you looked at it. Both of his shoes and socks ended up on the rug.

"Do you enjoy playing strip Shafskopf," he said as he dealt.

"Sometimes."

She scanned her cards gloomily. Terry took the last trick, ten of diamonds over the nine of hearts, to take the hand. Cindy tossed an earring onto the sofa.

"You're undressing me," she purred.

Terry trembled with anticipation.

Got to say something. Anything. Got to keep this going.

"Did you know that Schafskopf was invented by Bavarian shepherds?" was all he could offer.

"Really?"

I don't know if I can go through with this. I don't do strange! I don't do strange!"

Every woman, even a spy, needs a little something. Just a nano-ounce of something. Call it romance, emotion, excitement, or conflict, even an atom of normality. *Anything.* But not unremitting strangeness.

The gnarliest, thorniest cactus needs a drop of water every hundred years. In Milwaukee, this is sometimes lacking.

Terry got no-schnitzed on the next hand. Feigning disgust, he tossed his ring on the floor, along with one sock. The feel of his bare foot rubbing against the carpet excited him.

"I'm gonna use the bathroom, Terry. Deal while I'm gone. And don't cheat."

He brought out two more beers while she was gone.

The next several hands went badly for Cindy. Her other earring and her ring ended up on the pile. Terry madly recomputed.

I'm too far ahead. Have to toss a few.

He played the next hand clumsily, leading the ten and ace of diamonds to see them taken by jacks.

"Terry, what are you doing? You're getting drunk."

Could you make it more obvious? Why don't you just drop trou?

"I took a chance," he mumbled, as he tossed his other sock onto the sofa.

"Took a chance? You thought all the queens and the jacks had disappeared?"

They both were quiet as Terry dealt the next hand. He was about to reap a luxuriant harvest.

They played carefully. Cindy pondered her cards between sips. She finally played the king of spades. She stretched back as Norris took it with the ten of spades. His eyes darted from her chest to her lap.

"You're beating me, Terry," she said softly.

A vein started to throb near his temple. She inspected him again. Terry's heart was pounding. He took the last three tricks. When they counted, he'd won by two points.

"Terry!"

Cindy pretended to be dismayed. She reached into her blouse to unhook her bra. Terry looked away as she slipped it down her arms.

"Terry! I don't have much left. You have any music?"

He jumped up.

"What do you like?"

"The Righteous Brothers?"

"Yeah. I got it."

She turned down the lamp even more as "Unchained Melody" started to play. She smiled at him as he dealt.

All right, Terry. Let's see if you can get the job done.

Terry's hand was a disaster, all low cards. For a moment he panicked.

If I get no-schnitzed, it's double. I can't just sit here in my shorts. When do I make my move, for God's sake?

He played carefully, lost badly, but managed to get schnitz.

Cindy watched with interest as he peeled off his undershirt. It was as she feared.

A bony, almost skeletal chest. But not beyond redemption. Depending . . .

She watched him deal. Terry's up cards were all trump. Cindy's were all low.

"I think you're beating me, Terry," she said softly.

She slid down slightly into the sofa as she looked at her hand. Terry trembled. He sucked out her few trump cards. She struggled to take three tricks, barely making schnitz.

"What should I take off, Terry?"

Blood almost spurted from his ears.

"I don't know. Whatever you want."

Cindy slipped her hands under her skirt. She slid off her panties and tossed them onto his shirt.

"My turn," she said, as she started to deal. "I have only two things left, Terry. You better lose this one."

Terry could barely hold his cards.

What am I going to do? I can't win this one. I can't have her sitting there in just her blouse or just her skirt. Too early to make my move. I've got to lose this one.

Absolute catastrophe struck. Terry had all four queens, the highest trump. And as it turned out, he also had all four jacks. And a couple of aces for good measure. Not only couldn't he lose this, but Cindy might not even take a trick, no matter what he did.

He became clammy.

What do I do? I'm not drunk enough. Maybe she isn't either. She'll be sitting there while I have my pants on. Why doesn't she make a move?

He played as badly as he could. She still took only one trick. Didn't come close to schnitz.

"But, Terry."

She sat forward, knees together, ankles wide apart. Her blouse was wide open. The soft music floated through the room.

"I only have two things left on. And now you won them both."

Her voice was soft.

"What should we do?"

He froze.

I'm dead.

She glared at him.

Look, Ratso. You need the invite in Braille? I'm giving it to you in Braille.

Terry was terrified.

It's right here! Right in front of me. The real thing! What do I do? Can't think. I know! I'll deal quick, lose, and tell her we take it off together. But got to say something. Can't look too eager. Something scientific.

"You know dogs?"

He sped dealt.

"When they, like, have to go to the bathroom? They align themselves with the polar."

He grabbed his cards.

"What?"

What, I dangle it in your face, and I get dogs in the alley? This I won't put up with! I don't do strange! As God is my witness, I won't do strange!

"Like the magnetic axis."

She buttoned her blouse and grabbed her clothes.

"I don't do strange!" she screamed. *"I'm out of here!"*

"No! NO! Please! Stay. Let's . . ."

She had the door open.

"Fuck you! I . . . will . . . *not* . . . do . . . strange!"

"Shut up!" a voice shouted from a window next door. "I'm sleeping! Show some respect!"

"Respect my ass!"

Cindy held up her finger as she walked away.

"I'm out of here!"

Chapter Twenty-Five

General Li Yu looked at the officers sitting around his conference table. He was angry. No one dared to speak. They sat in silence for a long time.

"The honey trap failed," he said. "She was unsuccessful in seducing her target."

"How is that possible? Did he suspect her?"

"It's not clear. Our initial report is that she became frightened. Or disgusted."

"Forgive me," said an older colonel. "But she does not appear to be the kind of woman who is frightened or disgusted by anything."

"It's unclear. The venue is pathological. She was arrested for screaming in the street and making an obscene gesture."

"Did she reveal her identity?"

"No. She was given a ticket and paid a fine."

"What do we do now?"

The general paused to consider the question.

"The boy, Weber, and his uncle are helping a political candidate. We have his schedule. They will appear at a church festival in Milwaukee this weekend. We will have a man follow them."

"His orders?"

"We expect the woman who pretended to be the reporter will still follow them. We exposed her, and they have rejected her. But we have not yet been able to locate her. The boy is the bait. She will follow him, and our man will neutralize her."

"May he have more success than our last man, Chang Sheng."

"He is much tougher, and much more experienced than Chang Sheng" the general said. "A woman alone will have no chance against him."

"And then?"

"And then, a plane will land in the Milwaukee airport. A commando team will seize the boy and conceal him on the plane. The flight plan will be to Vancouver. And then to Beijing."

"We will snare the bird with the decoy. And then, the little monkey will be ours."

The officers around the table nodded.

Chapter Twenty-Six

Our posse— me, Bernie, Jimmy, and Trixie—gathered at the entrance to the parking lot of Saints Cyril and Methodius Catholic Church on South 15th Street. We were there to shake hands and drop lit at Pierogi Fest, the parish's annual fundraiser. Trixie was big on the church festivals, where everyone is a voter.

"So here's the plan," she said. "Joe, you and Bernie work the food stands. You drop lit and go 'Alderman Fieblewicz is on the grounds. We're here to say hello.' Jimmy, you and me, we'll work the picnic tables. Move it along. Thirty seconds a skin. Max."

We all nodded. Trixie was the quarterback and we followed her game plan.

"But you might get flak," she said. "Some morons might go like 'There shouldn't be politics in church.' Probably Flores supporters. To bust your chops. So you go, 'It's okay with the pastor.' See. They back off. And they never check. Okay?"

We nodded.

"Okay. Hit the beach."

There was a big crowd for Pierogi Fest. There always is. Pierogi are these little dumplings they fry in butter and onions. They fill them with sauerkraut or parsnips or cheese or whatever. They're damned good. I could eat a tray of them myself.

And they get plenty of folks from outside the parish. Plenty of families from the suburbs come to the fest to load up. Even a Chinese man with a camera stood about twenty feet away with his back to us. He was taking pictures of the church. You have to be careful not to waste lit. If they look suburban, or out of town, you go "Hi" and move on. You don't waste lit on nonvoters in Jimmy's district.

Bernie and I hit the first pierogi stand, run by the Ladies Archdiocesan Guild. They specialize in the sauerkraut and the cheese. My favorites. We started to work the long line.

An attractive woman in a sun hat and large sunglasses sat unnoticed at the farthest table from the food booths. Audrey Knapp kept an eye on the Chinese tourist as she pulled out her phone to text.

Stand by. Thirty minutes?

Or less.

The Chinese tourist started to walk slowly toward her. A stout man wearing a sash that said "Polka Police" grabbed his arm. He had a large, friendly face under a blond crewcut.

"Are we having fun yet?" the blond man bellowed.

The Chinese man stiffened. His hand went into his right pocket. The blond man blew a whistle. A smaller, older man standing nearby started to play "In Heaven, There Is No Beer" on his accordion. The blond man seized the tourist and tried to force him into an awkward polka.

A small crowd gathered around and sang "That's why we drink it here . . ."

The Chinese man started to knee his partner in the groin, and then thought better of it. When the song stopped, the man with the whistle mugged for the crowd.

"Five dollars to the parish. For not having fun yet."

The Chinese man stood impassively.

"Five dollars, or you go to jail. In the kitchen. You stuff pierogi."

The Chinese man slowly withdrew his wallet and handed him five dollars. The Polka Policeman walked on to the next victim.

As they worked the tables, Trixie and the alderman came closer to Audrey. She stood up and strolled farther away from them, toward the church. When she looked back, the Chinese man had disappeared.

Occasionally, one of the ladies went into the church with an empty tray and emerged with a full one. Audrey followed one of them. She got just beyond the beer tent when she felt metal jammed in her back.

"It has a silencer. If you scream or move quickly, they will not hear the shot. You will fall to the ground. I am a doctor, of course. I will tell them to call emergency and make your corpse comfortable while they wait. I will disappear."

"What do you want?"

"To talk to you. Walk toward that door."

They walked slowly in tandem. As they got to the door of the church, the priest came out.

"Father!"

Audrey threw her arms around his neck and turned sideways.

"I have happy news! My friend wants to convert!"

"Thank the Lord," the priest said.

He was in his sixties, with a good-natured expression and thick, graying hair. He put his hand on the man's arm.

"My great uncle was a Maryknoll missionary in China in 1949. He suffered greatly. His work is now bearing fruit. Welcome, my son."

The Chinese man inclined his head stiffly.

"We have a course of instruction. There are three works I strongly recommend you read."

"I'll be going," said Audrey.

She turned and ran into the church.

The priest still held the Chinese man's arm.

"*The Confessions of St. Augustine. Seven Story Mountain.* And Aquinas's proof of the existence of God, my son. Up until now, you have been immersed in a godless culture. A world without a sun. Welcome."

"I must use the bathroom," said the Chinese man.

"Inside and to the right. I am Father Philip. Please see me before you leave to receive your materials."

The Chinese man ran into the church. It was empty. He barely looked at the magnificent stained-glass windows, the stations of the cross below them, and the tabernacle and altar in the front.

He ran back to the stairs, which led down to the basement. He drew his weapon and walked carefully down the stairs into a large room. Two ten-foot wooden statues of St. Joseph and the Blessed Virgin Mary lay on their sides. Notes were pinned to each: "Hold for painter." A few painters' tarps were folded neatly between them. Trays of pierogi, covered in wax paper, were laid out on tables at the perimeter.

There was no one else in the room. As he started back up the stairs, he heard a noise. He stood back in the corner and covered his weapon with his other hand.

A plump woman in her sixties, wearing a hairnet and plastic gloves, carried three empty trays down the stairs. She paid no attention to the man in the corner. She emerged in a moment with a full tray of pierogi and went out.

The man was starting up the stairs when he heard another noise. Another woman in a hair net holding empty trays high in front of her walked down the stairs. As she passed him, she threw the trays at him and fired.

The man fired back as he fell. The bullet blew through a pierogi tray. Audrey stood over him and tased him until he stopped twitching. She knelt down to plunge a syringe into his arm.

He lay frozen. She dragged him down the rest of the stairs by his ankles and laid him out between the statues. She covered him with a tarp.

A white truck with "Prime Movers" on the side had pulled up outside the church. Two men got out. One of them carried a large cloth sack. As they started to enter the church, a kid with bushy red hair stuck his head around the corner.

"Here for the statues, Mister?"

"Yeah. Beat it kid. Nosy kid. We've got work to do."

The kid disappeared. The men went into the church and came out a minute later. One of them had the sack draped over his shoulder. A hand dangled out.

The kid popped his head around the corner again.

"Who's that, Mister?"

"St. Cyril."

"I saw his arm move."

"It's a miracle. I said beat it, kid."

They threw the sack into the back of the truck, jumped into the cab, and drove away.

Chapter Twenty-Seven

Lathrop Willis and Wayne Hawkin sat at a wooden table in Mory's on York Street in New Haven. A waiter appeared.

"A Red Cup, please."

"Yes, Sir. Anything else?"

"Not presently."

Willis ran his hand over the carved names on the table when the waiter left.

"I want to update you on Project Sif. The Republicans won't fund it, and the Democrats won't fight for more military spending. So, we're at a stalemate on the space issue with the Chinese. As long as neither of us has weapons in space, we dominate. But when and if that changes, we're very vulnerable."

"Why did we let them put Jade Rabbit on the moon?'

"Because we have weak leadership. In Congress and in the White House. They've lost the fire for American ascendancy. Perpetual American ascendancy. I told Lamar to shoot the damned thing down. Force the Speaker and the president to grow a pair. Nothing the Chinese could have done about it. Issue a modern Monroe doctrine. No nation besides ours will colonize space. But he didn't have the horses."

"Now, Iran and India are launching space probes."

"Absurd. They can't feed their own people. Have their hands out all the time. Every tribal victim state with a few scientists we educated at MIT or Caltech suddenly wants to be in space and have nuclear weapons. With technology they steal from us. We need to put a stop to it. Requires strong leadership."

"Your Cup, Sir."

The waiter placed a large pewter vessel, much larger than a chalice, on the table in front of them. He laid a linen towel next to it. Willis picked it up.

"*Pocula elevate. Nunc est bibendum.*"

He took a long drink of the sweet rum, Grenadine, and club soda.

"The nectar of the gods, Hawkin."

He wiped the rim with the towel and passed the cup to Hawkin.

"*Bibemus*," said Hawkin.

He, too, drank deeply.

"Of course yu've heard about what happened to Yin Hou?"

"He died. But how? Don't have the details."

Willis drank again.

"Human flesh search. The Chinese love to gang up on somebody. It started out a while ago when somebody was in the news for killing an animal. The blogs and emails hounded them to death. When you have more than a billion people, even a small percent of them constantly attacking you and publishing your address gets to you. Sometimes, they commit suicide."

"So, Yin Hou's a suicide?"

"No. The government picked up on the technique and probably twenty million people got whipped up to go after him. They finally found him hiding in a hut, sobbing. He had nowhere to go. Look at this. Carroll Dalton sent it to me. They preempted time on Chinese national TV for it the other day."

Willis handed the video on his phone to Hawkin. A Chinese general sat speaking behind a desk, flanked by two Chinese flags. English subtitles crawled underneath.

"Today, the government has announced the arrest and conviction of Professor Yin Hou for drug use, womanizing, leading a dissolute and depraved life, and treason. Upon hearing the report of his treachery, workers and students throughout China broke into angry shouts that stern judgment should be meted out to the anti-party, counterrevolutionary factional elements. In the echo of these shouts, a special military tribunal was held last week against the traitor for all ages, Yin Hou. The accursed one brought together undesirable forces and formed a faction as the boss of a modern-day factional group and committed such hideous crimes as attempting to overthrow the state by all sorts of intrigues and despicable methods with a wild ambition to grab the supreme power of our party and our state. All the crimes committed by the accused were proved in the course of the hearing and were admitted by him. A decision was read out at the trial. Every sentence of the decision rang like a hammer blow from our angry workers and students on the head of Yin Hou, an anti-party counterrevolutionary factional element and despicable political careerist and trickster. Yin Hou, who was worse than a dog, perpetrated thrice-cursed acts of treachery in betrayal of such profound trust and warmest paternal love shown by the party and the leader for him."

Willis turned off his phone.

"That was General Li Yu, speaking of careerists and tricksters. Dalton said that Hou was likely shot by a firing squad before the trial. We're confirming now."

"Firing squad?"

"Yes. Machine guns. Some of their younger soldiers like to see the target twitch—really blast the hell out of them. Sort of a reward, really. Keeps their minds off of women. Not enough to go around."

"How does Dalton know?"

"Code words. 'Thrice-cursed' and 'worse than a dog' are rarely used to describe senior officials. And occasional use of the past tense. Usually means pre-trial execution."

"What about Violet Light?"

"Don't know yet. Deeply encrypted with their new technique. No chatter about it other than the comment from Yin Hou. What progress is Maynard Gieck making on the Riemann hypothesis? Should be our best chance of breaking through and reading their traffic."

"He's doing his best. We're working with NSA mathematicians and a few academics. But it's slow."

Willis drank again.

"What's happening with the boy in Milwaukee?"

"Nothing, really. I'm more worried about that than you seem to be."

"Preposterous. The boy's just a numbers savant. Helpful in the past, but of limited use to us now. I'm not convinced he has the ability to do deep math. You really think they're still after him, don't you?"

"As a matter of fact, I do."

"Then, let the FBI handle it. Or the Milwaukee police."

"They can't. Don't have the expertise."

"Well then, Milwaukee will have to defend itself. Organize a militia. Don't imagine they have one, do they? The whole idea's absurd."

Willis signaled the waiter for the check.

"I love coming back to New Haven to recruit, Hawkin. New Keys men for the agency. And to the tables down at Mory's for a Red Cup. But time to get back to Langley."

Chapter Twenty-Eight

When we got to the Azteca on Oklahoma Avenue, Trixie was talking with Jimmy Fieblewicz and some thin guy. Frannie and I joined them, while Bernie sat to one side, typing on his iPad.

"So here's the deal," Trixie said. "This is Bautista Fragoso. Bautista is giving us advice on what to do at the Latin American Unity Conference. He isn't too thrilled about Santiago Flores. But he can't go public. That's why we're here."

"Correct. I am happy to help you, but it must be behind the scenes."

The guy seemed okay, but I couldn't get a read on him.

"So, Bautista," Trixie went on, "when Jimmy speaks to LAUC next week, what's the best way to connect? Get through to everybody. I mean personally, not just his issues speech."

Baustista nodded.

"Right. First of all, he has to be himself. He has to look like he wants to be there. Then, he has to say a few words in Spanish. And it has to sound halfway decent—not just political Spanish."

"Okay," said Jimmy.

"And it has to be about something that shows he wants to connect."

"Like what?"

"Pick out some food you like. You like huevos rancheros?"

"Yeah."

"Okay, then. Say *Lo que me gusta comer mas que nada son huevos rancheros.*' What I like to eat more than anything are eggs with red sauce."

"What? I'll never remember that."

"It's okay," Frannie said. "I got it."

"Frannie has to sign off on any foreign words," Jimmy said. "I got burned once —not by you—but they set me up. Frannie's a Spanish teacher. She has to sign off."

We all nodded.

"So, the Latino culture has kind of a macho element to it," Bautista said. "You know, boxing, things like that. I heard you have a black belt in karate?"

"Yeah. I mean, you sign up for an eight-week course at this place in the mall, and they guarantee you a black belt. And there's a six-week program. I'm halfway . . ."

"That's enough, Jimmy."

Trixie cut him off.

"He has a black belt."

"So, I'd tell them that, then give your speech."

Bautista got up to go.

"I've got to be careful. But a lot of people have a problem with Flores and the whole alderman piece. They can't come right out for you, but you'll get some votes."

"Bautista, I'll call you," Trixie said. "Thanks."

"So, here's the plan," she said, when he left. "Next Saturday, we go to Madison. It's a big day. The Democratic State Convention. You speak to LAUC at one in the afternoon. Then you grip and grin, mingle, mingle, mingle for a while. At three, we go to delegate selection. You get selected. At five, we put out a release. Says Jimmy killed in Madison. Juiced up LAUC. Picked as a delegate. The hero, see?"

"But what if they pack the house at LAUC?" I said. "They bring in the bad boys. They boo Jimmy. Then what?"

"Doesn't matter, Joe."

Trixie tried to be patient.

"It's all about squeeze. No such thing as bad squeeze. Only bad is no squeeze. We'll have two releases ready. If Flores empties the county jail and brings his supporters, Jimmy still kills. He shows courage. He attacks Flores. Stands up to the booing."

"Attacks him for what?"

"Immigration. Flores is bad for undocumented workers. He'd send them back."

"What? His uncles are undocumented."

"But he can't say that, can he? He can't rat on them. Look, what matters is what people read and hear."

Trixie saw we were skeptical.

"Trust me. We can't lose on this one. What can go wrong? Frannie vets everything he says in Spanish. I vet everything he says in English. And he can't go extemp."

She turned to him.

"Jimmy! No extemp!"

"Got it."

"What could possibly go wrong? Now, let's hit some doors. Finish up the ward."

As we were walking out, the manager came up to us.

"Is one of you Trixie LaFond?" he said.

"That would be me."

"I have a message for you. We got a call. Someone wants to meet you at Winners tonight at seven."

"Who was it?"

"I don't know."

"Man or woman?"

"I don't know. The barista who wrote it down already left."

"Okay. Thanks."

Trixie turned to us.

"Let's hit it. Jimmy, meet me at Winners at eight. I want to go over message for Madison."

"Okay."

Chapter Twenty-Nine

Yan Shifan sat at his desk, staring out the window. General Li Yu sat across from him, not saying a word. An older man in a suit and blue tie sat next to Li Yu. He also said nothing.

"General, meet Professor Zhu Sheng," the leader finally said. "It was he who discovered the proof of the Riemann Hypothesis. You will recall that we had mistakenly thought the honor went to Professor Yin Hou. But we were wrong."

The general nodded.

"I have provided Professor Sheng with the results of your surveillance of the boy in Wisconsin. Weber. The review of his computer. His notes and his work on the proof. Professor Sheng is alarmed at the progress of the boy's work."

Li Yu didn't respond.

"Professor Sheng will now explain the cause of his alarm."

"If I may," Sheng said, "I will give the background. For the purposes of cryptology, it is not enough simply to prove the hypothesis. Although that is difficult enough. It had never been proven by anyone until the Uighur . . . until I proved it."

He paused.

"It is also necessary to invent a cryptologic method for using the proof once it is found. In theory it is possible, but it is not apparent until you have the proof itself."

"Tell him what the boy has done," Yan Shifan said.

He was getting impatient.

"The boy has duplicated and then gone beyond the unpublished work of Bernhard Riemann, which was not known until long after his death."

"If it was unpublished, how is it known now?" said the general.

"Most of Riemann's notes were burned by his housekeeper. But his wife saved some, and they were deposited in a university. They are almost unintelligible. For many years, people assumed they were unimportant. He also made notes in a black book on a trip to Paris. That book has never been found."

"The point of all this?"

Yan Shifan showed his irritation.

"What has the boy done?"

"Some mathematicians think that Riemann worked out a proof and was about to publish it when he died. I will try to keep this simple. The key to his hypothesis is that all zeroes must lie along a critical line defined by the hypothesis. If you find a single zero that doesn't lie along the critical line, the hypothesis is false."

"So?"

"Before Riemann's notes were deciphered, mathematicians could only prove that the first one hundred thirty-eight zeroes were on the line. Riemann's notes showed a method to determine that the first thousands of zeroes were on the line. Using his methods, computers can now show that billions of zeros are on the line."

"You haven't told us what the boy has done."

"The boy's work shows a method to determine two things. First, that an infinite number of zeroes are on the critical line."

"We have been briefed on that already. As I understand it, that does not prove that all zeroes are on the critical line."

"That's true. But he has now gone farther. He has now proved that *all* zeroes up to an unknown number *n* are on the critical line."

"What's the point?"

"The point is that he is close to proving the hypothesis. The technique to go from 'All zeroes up to an *unknown number* are on the line' to

'*All* zeroes *must* be on the line' will occur to him quickly. And one other thing."

"What?"

"This line of attack on the proof also leads immediately to its adaptation in cryptology, one that no other government has the knowledge to penetrate."

"And you think the boy found this on his own?"

"I do. Unless he has discovered the black book that was lost in Paris in 1860 or went back in time and retrieved the papers from the housekeeper's fire."

Sheng regretted the joke as he spoke. The leader's face hardened. In some countries, it is dangerous to be a wiseass.

"That will be all," he said quietly.

"Thank you. I apologize."

Sheng darted out without looking at Li Yu.

"An insolent dog," said Yan Shifan. "But we can't shoot everybody. He abstains from liquor and women. His tongue doesn't wiggle. But tell me, you have not been successful in Milwaukee. Why?"

"It is a city with a defective culture, very unlike ours. Difficult to penetrate."

"We've lost two men. Experienced men. Their tracking chips were removed. This is not the work of Milwaukee."

"Correct. A woman is protecting him. She must have the support of their agency."

"A woman alone? And she caused the disappearance of our men?"

"Perhaps not by herself."

"What is your plan?"

"I'm sending in a team of men," the general said. "They will be disguised as tourists and students. They will follow the boy and the woman much more thoroughly. They will eliminate her and deliver the boy to the airport for the flight to Vancouver."

"Why not just eliminate the boy?"

"Excessive risk. We have caused them to distrust the woman. Without her, they are not taking precautions on their own. It should be a simple matter to get him to their airport."

"You cannot fail. Violet Light is well on its way to completion. If the Americans discover it, they will take it out militarily. That must not happen."

"It will not happen."

"Good."

Yan Shifan walked over to the door.

"Meilin!"

A young girl appeared instantly.

"A bottle of Armenian brandy. And two glasses, for myself and the general."

"At once, Sir."

Chapter Thirty

Trixie LaFond walked into Winners a little after seven. All eyes from those at the bar briefly scanned the cougar, like bumble bees mistakenly alighting on an orange golf ball that slowly rolls to a stop on a fairway. They immediately realized their mistake and looked away in search of more fragrant flowers.

Trixie glared at them.

Bite me rightly.

She threw back her shoulders and walked up to the hostess, who looked at her without enthusiasm.

"One? You might be more comfortable at the bar."

"No. I'm here to meet someone. Is there a man at a table waiting for someone to join him?"

"No. I'm afraid not."

"Too bad. Is there a woman?"

"No . . . actually yes. Yes, there is. In the corner."

She pointed into the next room.

"Is that her?"

"That's her."

Trixie headed across the room, past the usual wildlife in the Winners rainforest.

She marched up to the table and stood over Audrey Knapp.

"What do you want, lady? Joe told me about you."

"I want you to sit down and listen to me. It's important."

A waitress came to the table. She looked at Audrey.

"Can I get you a drink?"

"Two glasses of Pinot Noir."

Trixie sat down.

"Who are you?"

"My name is Audrey Knapp."

"Last time you said it was Janet Bachman. Are you a hooker?"

"No. Now listen to me. And listen good. I'm a mathematician. I work for the government. We know about Bernie's ability with math. I was at the contest that he won in Madison."

"Look lady. I've been working campaigns for a long time. Fatal attractions, fraud artists, thieves, your general troublemakers. And that's just the candidates. Folks who hang around campaigns are worse."

"Listen to me good! Bernie's in a lot of trouble."

"We don't need you, Lady. And we don't need Bernie. You know why? Because *we don't need trouble!*"

"Listen to me!"

Audrey grabbed Trixie's wrist. Trixie was silent.

"I am deadly serious," Audrey said. "The math that Bernie's doing breaks codes. It will break a Chinese code. The Chinese murdered one boy who discovered it. They are now trying to kill Bernie. And me. See? This isn't about an alderman campaign in Milwaukee."

Alderman Fieblewicz walked into the bar while the two women were talking. He sat on a stool.

"What'll you have?"

"Bottle of Miller."

He stuck out his hand to the man sitting next to him.

"Hi, I'm Jimmy Fieblewicz. The alderman."

The man shook his hand.

"Yeah."

"I'd like your vote. Running for reelection. I'm for jobs. And the phonics."

"Might be all right."

"Good."

He turned to the man on the other side of him.

"Hi, I'm Jimmy Fieblewicz."

Audrey threw some money on the table.

"I'm leaving. Trixie, here's what I want you to do. Call Joe Weber and tell him I want to meet him. And Officer Piano. Soon! And, I want you to do one more thing."

Audrey took out a pen and picked up a napkin. She wrote a phone number on it and gave it to Trixie.

"This is a number Joe can call. It's the agency I work for. It's not listed anywhere. When they answer, they won't identify themselves. Tell Joe not to lie about who he is. He should ask them if Audrey Knapp is an employee of the agency. They will check him out and call him back. When they do, all they'll say is that I'm an employee."

She stood up.

"Joe has my number. You must talk to him. And he must do as I say."

Trixie watched Audrey walk away. She drained her glass. When she saw Fieblewicz, she picked up Audrey's untouched glass and walked over to the bar.

She clinked Jimmy's bottle, and they both drank.

"What you got, Trix? Wassup?"

"Nothing. I'm too tired for message. Been a strange day. Crazy strange. Let's just relax."

"I think I'll work the bar."

He stood up.

"A vote's a vote."

"Bad idea to campaign in bars, Jimmy. They're drunks. They cause trouble. And anyway, they don't remember. Plus, most people here aren't in your district."

"They will be when I run for mayor next time."

He walked down to a man several stools away. He stuck out his hand.

"Hi, I'm Jimmy Fieblewicz, your . . ."

"I remember you, you moron."

The man extended his hand. When Fieblewicz reached to shake it, he pulled it away sharply. His companions howled.

"You voted for the pay raise at City Hall."

"You got the wrong guy. I wasn't there that day. I don't go down there much. It's a bad place."

"That's all right then."

A man with long hair at the end of the bar eyed Fieblewicz as he made his way down toward him. The man wore a green fatigue jacket with an insignia and "Ernie" sewn in black over the left pocket. He stood up when the candidate got to him.

"Hi. I'm Jimmy Fieblewicz, your hired hand."

"You running for politics?'

"Yes, I am."

The alderman looked at his jacket.

"Were you Airborne?"

"Every day."

The man could barely stand. His speech was slurred.

"I was in the army, too. Artillery. Nice to meet you. I'm running . . ."

"I'm gonna kick your ass."

"What?"

What the hell do I do? If he hits me, I'm in the paper. Trixie! Help!

Trixie walked up behind them. She stepped around Fieblewicz and stuck her chin out at the man.

"I got something to say to you. Jimmy, shake a few more hands and then come back here."

She stood looking up at the man.

"You know what I got to say to you?"

"What?"

"My man can kick your ass."

"No way."

"I just called the TV station. They're on their way down to watch him kick your ass and put it on TV."

"No way!"

"Yes, they are. Winner take all on the evening news. They'll be here in five minutes."

She squinted at his shirt.

"Either Ernie kicks Jimmy's ass, or Jimmy kicks Ernie's ass. You on?"

"Every day."

"Jimmy says you ain't much. TV didn't think you'd have the stones to do it. Stand over there by the window."

He looked at her.

"They need light to film it. And don't run away."

Ernie drew himself up.

"No way."

He marched over to the window and stood at attention, looking out.

Trixie walked back to Fieblewicz as he talked with two men at the bar.

"Jimmy! Time to go."

They walked out to the sidewalk.

"Where are you parked?" she said.

"Couple blocks away."

"I'm right here. I'll give you a ride."

Ernie was still standing at attention by the window, stone drunk. Trixie waved at him slowly. His mouth opened. She gave him the finger with both hands. He turned to lunge through the crowd.

"God, I love politics," she said.

She jumped in and pulled away quickly.

"It's all about the pipples. I love my pipples. Which block, Jimmy?"

Chapter Thirty-One

General Li Yu sat at his desk. He pressed a button.

"Is my call ready?"

"Yes, Sir. I'll connect you now."

In Madison, Wisconsin, six Chinese men sat around a conference table in the Concourse Hotel, waiting for the call. Three wore white lab coats. The others wore dark suits with no ties.

"Quan Ruxiu. Are you there?"

"Present, General."

"And you have the five other men with you?"

Quan Ruxiu looked around the table.

"Yes, General."

"The operation is set for Saturday. The primary target is the woman. The secondary target is the boy, Bernie Weber. You understand our priorities?"

"I do, General. But with permission, I would like to set out some information from my team."

"You have permission."

"Our primary assignment was to collect information on the start-ups and the university where we are employed. We have downloaded many of the formulas and production methods that the companies and the university falsely claim are trade secrets. We are close to completing the transfer of information on the new seed invention of the agricultural company, and the radar invention at the company I am assigned. Can this new assignment wait, or should we discontinue our efforts to complete the download?"

"Discontinue for now. The new assignment is urgent."

"We will do so."

"Here is the objective," the general said. "The Democratic convention is scheduled for this Saturday. An alderman from Milwaukee, named Jimmy Fieblewicz, will attend, accompanied by the boy. We expect that the woman will also attend to protect him. But we have exposed her to the boy's uncle and friends, and she is not welcome in their company."

"Will the boy and the alderman be alone?"

"No. The boy's uncle is always with him. Joe Weber. And there may be others."

"Do we know the alderman's schedule?"

"Yes. He arrives at the convention center this Saturday morning."

"And the woman?"

"She will almost certainly be there."

"Forgive me, but what is her name?"

"We do not know. There has been no traffic on her. She used the name Janet Bachman, but we know that that is false."

"Her appearance?"

"The only men who have seen her are missing. We do not know."

"Do we know the rest of the alderman's schedule?"

"Yes. At one, he will speak to the Latin American Unity Conference. After that, he will register as a delegate to their national convention."

"General, could you confirm our assignment and priorities?"

"Yes. Kill the woman. Leave no evidence. That is your first priority."

"And our next objective?"

"Take the boy. But only if you can do it without engaging the alderman and the uncle. That is secondary. Once the woman is out of the way, we will have no trouble taking him in Milwaukee and getting him out of the United States."

"It will be done, General."

"The last two men have disappeared. There are six of you. Do not fail."

"We will not fail."

Chapter Thirty-Two

I was driving Jimmy Fieblewicz, Trixie, Bernie, and Franny to Madison for the big convention.

"So, Jimmy . . ."

Trixie was giving Jimmy last word.

"The mark of an amateur in politics is that they say something and actually mean it. Don't go off message! Understand?!"

"Got it."

"I once committed the ultimate fox paws," she said. "I told that to a reporter off the record. The rodent published it. Said he didn't remember the off-the-record part. Even did a follow-up. They're always looking for a witch hunt on the eye of a gnat. So Jimmy! No extemp!"

"Got it. Definitely."

We pulled up into the parking lot of the Monona Terrace Convention Center. Frank Lloyd Wright designed it in 1938, but it almost didn't get built. The plans lay in a drawer for almost sixty years. People fought it over location, parking, impact. At one point, they thought they'd lost the drawings. And we're not talking plans by Ed the Carpenter here. We're talking Frank Lloyd Wright. They finally built it in 1997. Now, the Milwaukee posse was here to do business in Frank's building.

Chapter Thirty-Three

The phone rang. Madison Police Chief Lars Loftus picked it up. The caller ID showed a 202-area code.

"Hello."

"Chief Loftus?"

"Speaking."

"This is FBI agent Peter Bloom. I'm with the Washington, D.C., bureau of the FBI. I wanted to fill you in on an operation we're conducting that may have an impact in your jurisdiction. We'd like your help on it."

"Absolutely!"

Loftus's mustache quivered.

Something important! First time in the fourteen years I've been here! Not another weed bust at a fraternity, or a south side shooting by people from Chicago.

"We appreciate your help. This is confidential. Do I have your assurance that you will not share this information with anyone except on a need-to-know basis with the officers you assign to this?"

"Yes. Yes!"

"Good. There is an Asian drug gang that's based in Los Angeles. It's extended its operation to the Midwest. We have reason to believe that they are in Madison now. Two of our agents assigned to this will contact you presently. They'll describe the help we're looking for."

"Yes! Happy to help."

Maybe I can go FBI after this. I have the credentials. I'm a police chief. Movin' up to the big time!

"Thank you, Chief. That's outstanding. Good-bye."

Loftus leaned back in his chair. He thought of his favorite old movie, *The FBI Story*, with Jimmy Stewart.

Some serious butt kicked in that movie. Machine guns, kicking in the door, shooting. Good stuff. Not a cop in Madison, dressed in short uniform pants and a helmet, riding a bike down State Street, watching the loungers at the cafes mean mugging-him as he went by. No more going to grade schools dressed as Officer Buckle, the Safety Buffalo.

His secretary came on the intercom.

"Sir. Two gentlemen to see you."

"Do they have an appointment?"

"They're FBI agents."

"Bring them in!"

Loftus jumped up and ran to the mirror. He patted down the few hairs left on his head and smoothed his moustache. He threw back his shoulders and stood erect at the door. Two men in dark suits entered. They were exceptionally clean-cut, in their mid-twenties. He shook hands with each of them.

"Chief, I'm Agent George Stagl with the FBI. This is Agent Arthur Starr."

They pulled out their badges and offered them to Loftus for inspection. He waved them off.

"I've spoken with the D.C. Bureau. I know why you're here. Tell me how I can help you."

He showed them to chairs and sat down at his desk.

"Chief, this is highly confidential, as I'm sure our D.C. bureau told you."

"Yes. Yes."

"There is an Asian drug cartel operating out of LA. It's called the Lei Feng cartel. They are more efficient and more ruthless than the Mexican cartels. They've now come to the Midwest."

"Okay."

"Several of them are in Madison right now. They're here to recruit, set up a distribution network, and engage in identity theft. They steal credit card and driver's license information. Then they forge documents to get other cartel members into the country from China. Papers showing Madison, Wisconsin, raise much less suspicion than papers from New York or L.A., where the practice is widespread. These people are masters of deception and very cunning when it comes to selling their truth."

"Got it. What do you want me to do?"

"We are going to infiltrate and arrest these people. They are violent. We may have to subdue them. We would like you to send officers to the scene when we notify you and have your men take them into custody."

"Absolutely. Glad to do it."

"But one additional detail. We need to interrogate these people at the FBI facility in Virginia. We need you to hold them briefly, without booking them in your regular system. We will take custody of them for booking and transportation to Virginia."

"Well, I'd like to, but can I do that? Might have to talk to the City Attorney about how to make that work."

"Please don't."

`The agent was emphatic.

"The more this is discussed, the greater the likelihood of a leak. That would put our undercover men in danger."

"But is it legal?"

"It's the same as an extradition hold. You have my word that these men are wanted for federal crimes, which is our jurisdiction. They will be booked within twelve hours in Virginia."

"Well, I guess it's okay."

"It is. We've done this procedure with cooperating police departments in at least twenty other states."

"All right. I'll do it."

"Thank you, Chief. And could you give us your private cell number? We'll call directly. If you're available, we'd sure appreciate your taking custody of the criminals yourself."

"Absolutely!"

Loftus wrote down the number and handed it to him. They stood and shook hands.

"Thank you, Chief."

The two men left the Police Administration Building. They walked around the block to get in their vehicle, a white truck that said "Prime Movers" on the side.

Chapter Thirty-Four

We walked inside the Monona Terrace Convention Center. This was delegate selection week in Madison, time to select delegates to the Democratic national nominating convention.

Much depended on being selected. Fancy parties with free lobster and champagne. Celebrity sightings and the chance to meet famous politicians, to be interviewed on TV for local color.

Every four years, hordes from Eau Claire, Milwaukee, Ashland, Manitowoc, and all over Wisconsin compete to be selected as delegates, to escape for a brief moment and live the life they see on television.

A thousand people moved around in the convention hall. They were dressed in bizarre hats and jackets, pinned with dozens of buttons, all under signs for every political issue you could imagine.

"Welcome to the Democratic Convention," said the main banner.

Smaller signs covered the walls:

"A woman's place is in the House—and the Senate."

"If you can read this, thank a teacher."

"We are the 99 per cent."

"Is it true, or did you hear it on Fox News?"

There were also dozens of signs for every conceivable Democratic presidential candidate, Senate candidate, and candidates for the House and state legislature.

You have to understand something about Wisconsin. A political convention here is like a fair in medieval Europe where they sold feathers that fell off the Angel Gabriel at the Annunciation for a penny a piece. And the hucksters never run out of geese.

Of course, there was the usual assortment of red-dwarf political planetoids who form all governments, strutting to the praise of the rabble, convinced of their self-creation. But it was also a chance for ordinary people, trapped in numbing routines, to stand out from the crowd.

Ed Kitchen from Fond du Lac was there, covered in buttons that he sold for a dollar a piece:

"I read banned books."

"Friends don't let friends decapitate infidels."

Gunther Schmidt from Park Falls was there, with a small, wooden donkey secured to his head.

"Pull on the tail," he urged a man standing next to him.

The man pulled, and the donkey excreted a cigarette.

The three Lobermeir brothers from Minoqua were there, John, Joseph, and Leo, three bachelor lumberjacks who lived together in the woods. They walked single file in the room and even on the wide sidewalks of Madison, just as they did in the woods. Bernie squirmed a little bit as we walked through all this.

"Joe? Professor Lettow said I could go to the UW Math Department and use a computer while we're here. I'm getting close. Can I leave?"

"Some other time. Stick around."

Trixie said, "This way, Jimmy."

She took his arm and guided him to the right.

"Campaign manager's the hardest job in the world," she said to me. "Like trying to set up the starting line in a frog-jumping contest."

"How'd he do practicing his LAUC speech?"

"There aren't enough *O*s in 'smooth.' Jimmy kills."

A Chinese man in the middle of the crowd pulled out his phone and walked to the side.

"*Ni Hao.*"

"*Ni Hao.*"

"Where are you?"

"We are all at the Convention Center, as ordered."

"How many people are there?"

"Perhaps a thousand, General. It is beyond belief. It has all the super-stition of our New Year, lacking only paper dragons. But they actually pick their President this way."

"When you let the peasantry engage in politics, this is what you get. They are a diseased and disorderly culture. Hooliganism and parasitism and injury to the State occur when the rabble are permitted to do these things."

"You are right, General."

"They will disappear in a generation. Their people will hang them-selves with stolen dog leashes in the alleys of their ghettos. They will poison their starving families and roll them up in stolen carpets."

"You are right, General."

"Have you seen the woman?"

"No. The boy is here, with the uncle and some others."

"Find her. She will certainly be there. And eliminate her."

"Yes, General."

"*Zai Jian.*"

"*Zai Jian.*"

It was about a quarter to one when we walked into the side hall where LAUC was meeting. The room was full of people. Jimmy and Trixie started down the front row, shaking hands. The people were warm and friendly.

The leadership of LAUC sat at a long table on a stage in the front under a banner that said, "Latin American Unity Conference." Bautista Fragoso sat at the end. As I walked up to the front, he got up and left for the rear of the room.

A man came up to me to shake my hand.

"Mr. Weber? I am Juan Carlos Puga, the President of LAUC. We wish to welcome you and Alderman Fieblewicz."

"Thank you. Glad to be here."

I looked in the back of the room. Bautista Fragoso was standing with a group of men who kept looking over at us. They were laughing. Well, not much they could do. If this was a set-up, Jimmy would go to Plan B and attack Flores. Trixie had the bases covered. No possibility of error.

I went to sit with Franny and Bernie a few rows in. Trixie was in the back of the room, whispering with a woman holding a clipboard.

Jimmy Fieblewicz walked up to the lectern to get a feel for it. Bautista Fragoso came up to him.

"Alderman Fieblewicz, welcome. I want to show you our teleprompter."

"I got my speech on paper."

"Yes. I know. But when our guests use Spanish phrases, we ask that they read them from this teleprompter. It projects behind you, and the audience can follow your words. It's very important. There are many accents and dialects. Puerto Rican. Mexican. Honduran. Chileno."

He turned on the teleprompter. Jimmy took out his paper and compared all the words.

"Lo que me gusta comer mas que nada . . ."

They looked identical.

"Okay. I'll do it. But I read the rest from my paper, right?"

"Of course. I will stand next to you and activate the prompter only for the Spanish phrases."

Jimmy was still uneasy.

No extemp! No extemp!

He looked around for Frannie. She had gone to use the restroom. He looked for Trixie. She was standing just outside the door and talking with the woman with the clip board. He shrugged. The words looked the same. This wasn't extemp. It was okay.

"Okay. Good to go."

"Great."

Fragoso headed to the back of the room.

Juan Carlos Puga walked up to the podium, where he banged the hell out of an oversized gavel. Frannie came back into the room and slid in next to me. Trixie took a seat a few rows behind.

"*Bienvenidos a todos.*"

Puga stopped whacking the gavel. He kept speaking in Spanish, welcoming everyone, dignitaries by name, and acknowledging us.

"And it now gives me great pleasure to introduce our guest this afternoon, Alderman Fieblewicz of Milwaukee. The alderman is running for reelection. LAUC has not taken a position yet in this race, and we welcome the chance to hear from the alderman. He states that in his next term, he will fight for jobs, immigration reform, and health care. Alderman Fieblewicz."

Jimmy stepped up to the podium.

"Good afternoon. I am Alderman Jimmy Fieblewicz, and it gives me great pleasure to be here with you. Let me tell you a little bit about myself."

He went on a little too long about his background in politics. He finally put down his paper and nodded to Fragoso, who activated the teleprompter.

"What is this?" Frannie said.

She was alarmed. She took my arm. I looked behind me. Trixie was on her feet, her face tight and red. She sat down.

"*Lo que me gusta comer mas que nada son rancheros con huevos,*" Jimmy said.   His voice boomed as he smiled at the crowd.

The men laughed. The women sat like stones, arms folded, glaring at him. Shouts of "*payaso*" (clown) and "*burlador*" (joker) could be heard. "*Idiota*," a man shouted as he leaped to his feet.

Another man in a checked sport jacket jumped up from the front row. He wore tangerine shoes and a porkpie hat. He high-stepped smartly parallel to the stage. When he walked in front of Jimmy, he lifted his jacket, bent over, and gave a loud Bronx cheer. The crowd roared.He high-stepped back smartly in reverse, and again lifted his jacked and bent over when he was in front of Jimmy. The crowd clapped.

Poor Jimmy tried to finish his speech.

"I'm for job creation," he said, almost shouting over the laughter. "I'll work with small business . . ."

It was no use. People got up to leave. Others called out insults when he paused. He finally hung it up. He thanked them and hurried out the door.

Trixie took him into a small conference room across the floor. We all hustled in after him and closed the door. Trixie turned on him.

"So, what the *hell* do you think you're doing?" she said.

"What? What? Me? I just did what you told me! Frannie looked at the Spanish."

"I told you no extemp! Bautista screwed us! As God is my witness, I will get him. I'll have him reamed, steamed, and dry cleaned!"

"I just said what you told me!"

"No you didn't, Jimmy."

"What did I say?"

"You want the really, really bad news?"

"What?"

Frannie could hardly look at him.

"You said the thing you liked to eat more than anything were cowboys with balls."

144

"What? That's a lie!"

"Jimmy."

Frannie tried to control her tone.

"'Huevos rancheros' are eggs with red sauce. 'Rancheros con huevos' are cowboys with balls."

"But they're the same words!"

"In a different order."

"But the phonics?"

"Forget the phonics!"

Trixie almost screamed.

"I told you no extemp! *You have to have half a brain to do the triangulation thing*! "Forget the phonics! Never again! No more phonics. And no more triangulating!"

No one spoke.

"It'll be okay. It'll be okay."

Trixie tried to settle her nerves.

"Jimmy, you stay here and rest until delegate selection. We'll bring you a sandwich."

There was a knock on the door.

"Who's there?"

"Roland Cheek. Reporter from *The Milwaukee Journal*."

Trixie put a finger to her lips. We all shut up. She whipped open the door, stepped out, and pulled it shut.

"Who's in there?" Cheek said.

He was feeling pretty cocky about his bad self. He was no ordinary Jimmy Olson for the local papyrus scroll. He'd had strong snitching instincts from early childhood and had squealed on half the class by the fifth grade. Always sniffing like a dog on a log, sniffing until he flushed out the lizard.

Cheek had just received a local coverage award for his special at Christmas last year. He remembered every word.

"There have been security alarms at stores and malls. Merchants don't want people showing up drunk, or flash mobs, or shoplifting, or fighting over parking spaces. Remember, know who is hiding behind your car!"

He single-handedly drove mall Christmas sales down ten percent. He was feeling righteous. He would smoke out Fieblewicz's nasty, lying ass.

"It's our war room. What do you want, Roland?"

"How'd Jimmy do?"

"He killed."

"I heard he got killed. They threw him out."

"Bull."

"Santiago Flores's people told me."

He pulled out a pad.

"What do you think of Flores?"

"I like him. I heard he killed a man. But I like him."

"Come on, Trix. You got to give me something to write about. Need some meat."

"Flores? I was sorry to hear he was beaten up by a rival pimp."

"Come on, Trix. Something I can print. I need some meat."

"Bad dog. No meat for you."

"Look, Trix. We need each other. The more I know, the more your man's side of it's likely to get printed."

"I've heard that before."

He closed his note pad.

"See you at delegate selection, Trix."

Chapter Thirty-Five

Chinese agents were not the only uninvited guests at the Democratic convention. Two blocks off the square, close to the convention center, the failed lawyer but prominent lobbyist Scroggins "Scrod" Boston finished altering his office for the next visitors. The Democratic minority leader had just left. The Republicans had the next appointment.

Scrod liked to boast that he was a descendant of an old Boston family, even though he was born in Sheboygan, Wisconsin. When he was conceived, his father was seventy-five and his mother was forty-six.

Boston took down the picture of Barack Obama and hung a picture of Ronald Reagan. He turned around the sign that said, "Insurance companies are Republican death panels" so that it now said, "I'd vote for a Dem but I'm allergic to nuts." He turned around the other sign that said, "Abolish corporate personhood" so it now read, "Occupy a job."

He heard a knock.

"Come in."

He shook hands warmly with the three men who entered. They took seats around a conference table next to his desk. The oldest and most impressive was Faxton Hubbard, prominent in party leadership, and he looked the part with thinning hair, gin jowls, half glasses on his red-veined nose, and tufts of hair peeking from his ears and nose.

Next to Hubbard sat the sneaky-eyed, Pan-like Todd Venedig, another prominent Republican. Venedig was crafty, unctuous, and ambitious, but he couldn't feign sincerity, a death blow in politics. And so he mouldered, working behind the scenes.

The most disturbing of the three visitors was Mandrake, a handsome man in his late twenties who sat erect without smiling. Mandrake had never revealed a surname. He wore jeans with a dark blue shirt, and had his blonde hair combed down across his forehead. He was a dollar-a-year man, on loan from a think tank.

"Mandrake's folks had an idea," said Hubbard. "We're not going to be part of it, but he might need your help if it blows up, Scrod."

"Here it is," Mandrake said. "We know some of those delegates have drugs on them. I'm going to their convention undercover, and ID the folks who likely have them. I'll call in the police. If I think they've thrown them away, I'll slip a small stash in their pockets. They shouldn't be permitted to avoid justice that way."

"We're not having any part of this," Venedig said. "No part. Who you targeting?"

"I popped in a little while ago. There are more Asians there than usual. I may do them. Not onto a Myrtle of Kewaskum, if you know what I mean. Only bad folks who probably got scared and ditched it."

Hubbard and Venedig got up.

"We're leaving. We're not part of this. Tell Scrod what you might need if there's trouble."

"Okay. Scrod, here's the thing . . ."

Venedig and Hubbard left the office.

Chapter Thirty-Six

The flower of the Democratic intelligentsia was assembled to fight the Republicans. Chairing the Democratic delegate selection convention was Bucky Christiansen of Viroqua. Bucky was a big, noisy bullshitter, a former mortician who had become an interior decorator. His signature flourishes for living rooms were crimson satin pillows, a large stuffed trout on the wall, and pictures of Norway. As chair of the Rules Committee of the Vernon County statutory party, Bucky knew the rules, and, by God, he would enforce them.

The vice-chair of the convention was Emily Liszt, a Madison activist. The tips she earned working as Mistress Ursula the Dominatrix at the Velvet Hare on Mifflin Street supported her political habit.

Emily prowled the rear, clenching a wooden ruler, occasionally giving a stiff nod to her many clients among the legislators.

Bucky stood at the podium holding a gavel. He was dressed in a checkered jacket and khaki pants. He worked a toothpick as he surveyed the crowd.

Mandrake walked into the convention hall. Two ladies were seated at the registration desk in the corner. Several hundred canvas bags, loaded with campaign literature, platform pamphlets, and schedules of events, were stacked behind them.

"One guest credential," Mandrake said.

"Ten dollars."

One of the women handed him a blank nametag with a brown ribbon hanging from it.

"Print your name, and here's a bag of materials."

She handed him a canvas bag.

"Thank you."

Mandrake headed for a side door behind the women. As they helped the next guest, he scooped up five more bags and slipped out the door.

Bucky Christiansen banged the gavel.

"Hear ye! Hear ye! This meeting will come to order!"

He banged some more. The room quieted as the last delegates took their seats.

A half-dozen Chinese men were scattered around the room. From time to time, they looked over at Bernie and Joe Weber.

An attractive woman with Elton John-sized sunglasses and a floppy straw hat covered with campaign buttons sat in the back. She didn't pay any attention to Bucky.

"So here's the deal," Bucky said.

He pointed to a screen that said, "Delegate Selection."

"New rules. So, don't blame me. These just came down from the DNC."

He went to the next screen.

"Big change this year. Last time, we had seventy-five delegates elected based on how the candidate they supported finished in the Wisconsin Primary. We had some unpledged automatics—DNC members, Congresspersons, big-city mayors, and that. "

Bucky paused for the kill.

"Big change. This time, all delegates are unpledged. The Wisconsin Primary will only be advisory from now on. You get selected today, and you go to the Convention unpledged. You got plenty of power that way. The candidates will have to come into Wisconsin a ton to pay more attention to us."

Bernie started to shift in his seat.

"Joe," he whispered. "I'm gonna go to the bathroom and get a soda."

"Okay."

Bernie slipped out a side door. Two Chinese men stood up and walked out the back. The woman with the floppy hat got up and sauntered out the other side.

"And we got strong diversity requirements. The minimum is this. Fifty percent of the delegates have to be women. Ten percent have to be openly LGTB. And thirty percent have to be minorities. We don't count three-fers. We do count two-fers, but they're discouraged. This is just the minimum. We'll try to exceed this if we can."

He looked around.

"Any questions?"

There were none.

"You got to check one of the following categories when your come to the desk with your application: Caucasian male; African American; Asian/Pacific Islander; Hispanic; Native American; Caucasian female; two or more races; and then, gay/lesbian/bisexual/transgender; or Caucasian male LGBT. Any questions on that?"

Silence.

"Okay. We'll have two desks. I head the selection desk over there. What I decide goes on the party slate. You vote it up or down. I will be assisted by Johnny Dee of Mt. Horeb. Johnny?"

A man in a shiny black suit stood up with a big smile and nodded. Johnny Dee had snappy blue eyes. He wore a maroon pocket handkerchief, with a stickpin in his electric blue tie.

"The appeals desk will be run by Ursula, I mean Emily Liszt," Bucky said.

"You don't like what I decide, you appeal to Emily."

Emily also stood, and she and Johnny Dee remained standing.

"Emily will be assisted by Sparrow. Sparrow is an alder on the Madison City Council. Sparrow?"

An elf with a waxed Mohawk and waxed eyebrows stood up and nodded.

"And finally, the sergeant-at-arms will be Mr. Cattanaw of Neillsville. That would be the Catfish. Catfish?"

A man in jeans and a tee shirt that said "Burr Oaks Bowl" stood up. He had curly, sandy hair, and freckles. The crowd applauded the team.

"Okay. Line up. Desk opens in five minutes."

Out in the hall, a Chinese man approached Bernie.

"I apologize. You are student who won the mathematics competition. Yes?" the man said.

"That's me."

"I am having disagreement with two graduate students on problem. Could you resolve it?"

"Sure. What is it?"

"Two-color card problem."

"What's that?"

"You have four cards. Two are black and two are red. You put them face down and pick two of them at random. What is the probability that you will pick two cards of the same color?"

"What do your friends say?"

"One say two-thirds probability. The other say fifty-fifty probability."

Bernie thought for a minute.

"They're both wrong," he said. "The probability is only one-third."

"Can you explain that to them?"

"Yes."

"Come with me."

The man dialed and spoke in Chinese.

"The little monkey is ours. I am taking him away now. I will make him unconscious before I take him to another location."

"Do not arouse the barking of dogs. Have you seen the woman?"

"Yes. She has been observing us. She is following me now. But she is alone."

"Eliminate the whore. And report again."

The man put away his phone.

"My friends are ready. We will go to them."

He and Bernie walked down the hall.

Audrey dialed as she followed at a distance. A large man in the back of the room wearing a cowboy hat covered with buttons answered the phone.

"George? It's me. They have the boy. I'm going after them."

"Where are you? You're close."

"In the hallway outside. Follow me."

"On the way."

George Stagl's phone rang again as he stood up.

"Yes?"

"Agent Stagl? This is Chief Loftus. Returning your call."

"I didn't call you."

"I got a message from someone. It just said come to the convention center to arrest the Chinese people. The message said that they had drugs on them."

Stagl looked up. A blond man dressed in jeans and a dark blue shirt set a canvas bag behind the chair of a Chinese man. He carried two more.

"You're right. I misspoke. My team must have called. Come immediately. And there is another man with them. A blond man. In jeans and a dark-blue shirt. He may be carrying several canvas bags of materials. Arrest him, too. Then find me immediately."

"We're on our way."

Jimmy Fieblewicz took a seat in front of Bucky and Johnny Dee. Bucky looked over his application.

"What pronoun should I use for you?"

"What?"

"I don't know. Just reading here."

Bucky looked down again.

"You see, we got a problem here. We only got room for three Caucasian males from Milwaukee."

"Only three for all of Milwaukee?"

Bucky ignored the question.

"One of them is the head of the teachers' union. The other's the head of the public employees. We need message on the third. We got a guy who says he's a bear hunter. Gives good Second Amendment. Any pictures of you with a dead animal?"

"What kind?"

"Anything."

"Not really."

"You're not LGBT, are you?"

"Not really."

"You got any Indian in you?"

"Not really."

"Right. Okay. I see you're a blue-eyed gentleman. They're recessive, you know. You got any brown eyes in your family?"

"My mom's side. But they're more your Swabians, and your Appenzellers."

"Got it. Well you're out of luck. But I got something might help you."

Bucky pulled off a sheet from a pad. It said "DYNA-GENE CONTRACT."

"You mail them a swab from your cheek. They do a DNA. They have a contract with the party. Costs eighty-five dollars."

"What for?"

"You'd be surprised what they come up with. Last time, a guy named Danny Monahan wanted to be a delegate. He had blue eyes and sandy hair. DYNA-GENE did his DNA. Turned out he was two percent Argentinian Indian. Now, how the hell did that happen? But he made it."

"I'll think about it."

Fieblewicz walked slowly over to the appeal line as Trixie hurried toward him.

Chapter Thirty-Seven

The Chinese man took Bernie's arm outside the door and guided him toward another hallway.

"Excuse me. I must call my friends."

He dialed.

"*Ni hao*."

"*Ni hao*. Where are you?"

"With the boy."

"Can he understand?"

"No. And where are you?"

"Still in the hall."

"Come out now. I will take him to the arranged room. We will secure him and take him elsewhere."

"Are you being followed?"

"Yes. The woman. She wears a straw hat. Mid-thirties. Large glasses. Many buttons. Eliminate her."

"I will. I am leaving now. *Zai jian*."

The Chinese man in the convention hall stood up to leave. Bucky and Catfish walked in the aisle ahead of him.

"Bucky, we're noncompliant."

Catfish looked at his sheet.

"On what?"

"The minority piece."

"We gotta get us some."

Bucky walked up to the Chinese man as he was leaving.

"Son, want to be a delegate?"

The man shook his head.

"You a citizen?"

He shook his head again.

"You're legal though."

"Yes."

"Good enough."

Bucky gave him a card that said "Delegate receipt" with a number and Bucky's signature.

"You change your mind, give it to the girls at the desk. They'll give you your credentials."

"Okay."

"And one other thing, Son. Remember this. The time to plant corn is when the buds on the willow tree are big as a squirrel's ear."

People from Wisconsin assume that any third-world types they see in Madison are here to learn how to grow food.

The man nodded and left.

George Stagl's phone rang again.

"Audrey?"

"I need you out here. Now. I'm following the boy. Another one's behind me. And there are others inside."

"Right."

Stagl trotted to the door.

Bernie and his companion turned the corner into a side hallway. There were signs on each of the doors announcing meetings: Platform Committee, Empowerment Room, Administrative Committee, and several more.

"Where are your friends?" Bernie said.

"At end of hall. Near the door."

They walked down the hall.

"Bernie! Don't go with him! Go back to your uncle!"

Audrey ran toward him. The Chinese man reached into his jacket pocket.

"Run, Bernie! Run!"

"Joe told me about you!"

Bernie yelled back at Audrey and bolted into the Empowerment Room. The Chinese man ran in after him. A dozen women in the front of the room looked up as Bernie ran in, followed closely by the Chinese man. Audrey barged in a moment later.

Three signs hung on the wall in front: "Aggressors," "We've got spirit," and "Empower."

A small audience was seated on the side. Bernie sat in the front row of spectators. He kept peering over his shoulder. The Chinese man took an empty seat a few rows back. Audrey sat in the last row directly behind him.

The leader called for silence.

"We are the *aggressors*!" she said.

The others nodded.

"We will now watch a video from our Congressional leader, Nancy Pelosi."

Another Chinese man slipped into the room and stood near the door. It opened again, and a large man in a cowboy hat came in. He sat a few seats away from Audrey.

The woman in the front started a video of Nancy Pelosi, standing in front of a crowd of people on the steps of the U.S. Capitol.

"I am Nancy Pelosi. Standing behind me are most of the members of the Democratic caucus in the House of Representatives. I am very proud to announce that for the first time in American history, our caucus is less than fifty per cent white males!"

The room burst into applause.

"We will now try to understand the reasons for our past election losses," the woman in the front said.

Audrey suddenly stood up.

"I rise in sisterhood to speak!"

The room was quiet. Audrey pointed to the Chinese man sitting behind Bernie.

"This man is a human trafficker! He has come to kidnap teen runaways to work in massage parlors!"

This was a bullet into the Archduke Ferdinand. The pilot of a hijacked plane shouting "Allah Akbar!" over the intercom.

"Squad up!" shouted the leader. "General quarters!"

A dozen women from the front of the room and a few spectators ran over to the pervert to scream at him. He jumped up and slapped one of them. She collapsed as he ran for the door.

Audrey had a scarf over her hand. She reached through the melee to tase him.

The large man with the cowboy hat in the back row had his jacket over his hand. He tased the man near the door and jumped up.

"We are first responders!" he said. "Step back and let us do our work! We have called the police! Do not interfere!"

Audrey reached in her pocket and plunged a needle into her victim's arm as he spasmed.

"He'll be more comfortable now."

She hurried over to the other man and did the same.

Stagl was on the phone.

"Where are you, Loftus?"

"Looking for you."

"Side hallway. Get in here now. Room sign says 'Empowerment.'"

"Roger."

Audrey comforted the woman on the floor.

"We've called the police. They're on the way."

The door opened. Chief Loftus trotted in with six officers.

"These gentlemen need medical care."

Stagl pointed at the two unconscious men.

"Please take them to the van, Officer."

"Roger!" Loftus said.

This was the real deal. Never again would he be the Lutefisk King at Syttende Mai, or the geek in the dunk tank at the Lions Picnic. He would be Special Agent Loftus of the FBI.

Two officers stepped forward. They grabbed one of the men by the ankles and shoulders and ran him out of the room with him. Two more did the same with the other man. Outside, more officers were marching a handcuffed blond man in a dark blue shirt into the van.

"Don't hurt me!" Mandrake said. "Please don't hurt me!"

A couple of people were panhandling for coffee money nearby.

"The whole world is watching!" they said. "The whole world is watching! The whole world is watching!"

It did no good. The cops threw Mandrake into the van, along with the two unconscious Chinese men. Stagl jumped into the cab and drove away.

Chapter Thirty-Eight

Frannie and I stood with Jimmy and Trixie in the appeals line. We were the muscle. Trixie thought it'd be harder for them to turn him down in front of his posse.

"Where the hell is Bernie? I'm getting worried."

"Relax," Frannie said to me. "There's a big crowd here. What can go wrong?"

"Next."

Emily Liszt motioned to Jimmy to take a seat. We all moved in behind his chair. Emily almost sneered as she looked him over.

Another pale, pudgy one with no victim chops.

She tightened her grip on her ruler.

I'd love to spank him good and pink.

She frowned as she looked at his resume.

"It's difficult to see how chair Bucky erred here. I don't see anything to distinguish you from many other unsuccessful applicants."

Sparrow nodded vigorously. The waxed mohawk bobbed up and down.

"Come on!"

Trixie butted in.

"He's elected. A loyal Democrat for a long time. It'll help him in his reelection."

Emily Liszt and Sparrow smirked at each other.

"That's very special. But we must win elections on the issues. Being a delegate shouldn't be the focus."

Trixie started to lose it.

"What do you know about running a campaign? Ever done it?"

Emily Liszt smiled over at Sparrow.

"No."

"Then, what's the problem?"

"He doesn't give me what I need."

Sparrow tittered.

Trixie jumped up.

"We're out of here, Jimmy. Place is beyond belief."

Chapter Thirty-Nine

As his thoughts wandered, Mayor Peavey Snears stretched content-edly in an armchair in front of Chief Loftus's desk.

Beaudacious squeeze would come of this. The Wisconsin State Jour-nal, *at least two of the TV stations, all the radio. "Mayor cooperates in FBI sting. Takes West Coast drug cartel off the streets of Madison." They might even do a spec piece. "Mayor mentioned for Governor in next election."*

"Good work, Loftus," the Mayor said. "Outstanding performance. I've had my eye on you for a long time. You've never disappointed."

Loftus looked down modestly at his desk. He gently shook his head.

"Let's call them," Snears said. "We need to confirm that the ops are over. Our release goes out this afternoon."

Mayor Snears had once been on the outside, a Medusa-haired activist with a nest of Marley dried-cloth snakes on his head. He ran against the last mayor, branding him a corporate stooge. He won.

But once in office, Snears committed treason. He started to wear ironed shirts. He got a haircut. A hotel wanted to expand. Instead of tanking it instantly, he said he'd study it. Now, he had another Medusa-haired Marley wannabee with righteous dreads blasting Snears as a corporate stooge. Squeeze from the FBI sting might save his lying, corporate ass.

Loftus dialed. He put it on speaker.

"Hello?"

"Hello. This is Chief Lars Loftus of Madison, Wisconsin. May I speak with Agent Peter Bloom please?"

"Who?"

"Agent Peter Bloom."

"Just a minute."

He remained on hold for several minutes.

"Hello? Chief Loftus?"

"Yes."

"I'm afraid that isn't possible. Peter Bloom is gone."

"Where is he?"

"He died six years ago."

Loftus was afraid to look at the Mayor.

"Could I speak to George Stagl or Arthur Starr?"

"Just a minute."

Snears glared at him.

The receptionist came back on the line.

"Mr. Stagl retired three years ago. We don't know where he is. No one's heard of an Arthur Starr."

"Thank you."

Loftus hung up.

"Loftus. We let thugs kidnap a rival cartel in our city, run off with the drugs, and they disappear without a bubble? And your men load their truck?"

Loftus hung his head.

"Should I tell the alders?"

"No. *No!*"

Snears' tone went from angry to feline.

"The alders don't have the ability. The discretion to put this in the proper perspective. *They'll swoop down on a wounded animal. Sparrow will peck me a new one. They're ambitious. Greedy. Especially that prick with the dreads.* Think of all the good things we do, Loftus. If this gets out, citizens may be unnecessarily concerned."

"Of course. Of course."

"Think of it as a win-win, Loftus. You got rid of two cartels at once. They won't have the stones to come back. Good job, Loftus."

"Thank you, Mayor."

He stared out the window as the mayor left. He was still Chief Loftus. Still top crime dog in the Madison Police Department.

Chapter Forty

I sat with Frannie and Bernie at a table in Benji's, the deli just north of Milwaukee in the suburb of Shorewood.

"Okay, Bernie. What did she say exactly?"

"She said she has information for us. She's not what you think."

"No kidding. I thought she was Janet from the newspaper. Why isn't this a scam, too?"

Bernie squirmed a little.

"She said she told Trixie and to pass it on."

"She did tell Trixie. And Trixie thinks she's lying."

I saw the woman come through the door. She walked up to our table and sat down. Uninvited. Right next to me.

"What do you want?"

"Joe, listen to me. I'm out here to protect Bernie. The only reason I'm here. I work for a federal agency."

Bernie looked somber. Frannie put her hand on his arm.

"Which one?"

"None of your goddamned business. Listen to me. The Chinese are after Bernie. It's his Riemann breakthrough. It threatens their codes."

"What do you know about codes and the Riemann thing?"

"I have a PhD in math. Probably the only one in this deli. Let's cut the crap. They killed a kid who proved it, and they'll kill another kid who proves it."

"Even in Wisconsin?"

"Especially in Wisconsin. We have a team in place in Milwaukee to take them out."

"What's your name?"

"Audrey Knapp. Listen to me. You've got to protect Bernie. Use your friends in the Milwaukee Police. We'll need them."

"I don't believe you."

I was testing her.

"Yes, you do."

"Why do you say that?"

"You turned down the invitation for Bernie to go to China. Just like Janet Bachman advised you."

"How do you know that?"

"I know."

She got up.

"Stop being a jerk. And tell Jerry Piano I need to talk to him. When I call, he'll say fine, and he'll do what I tell him. There won't be any arguing."

"I'll think about it," I said.

Bernie didn't say anything.

"I'll leave you with this. We can stop them now. Bernie, once you finish your work, and it's published, it's too late for them. There won't be any reason to keep after you. But until then, be very careful. You have friends on your side. And I'm one of them."

Benji, with his friendly brown eyes and big smile, was walking over to take her order. She waved him off and left the restaurant.

Chapter Forty-One

Four men sat around a conference table in the Madison Concourse Hotel. The phone rang. One of the men pressed the speaker button.

"Quan Ruxiu. Are you there?"

"Yes, General."

"And you have three other men with you?"

"Yes, General."

"Last time you had five other men with you."

Quan Ruxiu shifted uneasily. The others stared at him without pity.

"Yes, General. They failed to take precautions."

"How could they have disappeared? And their tracking devices removed? From a clown convention in a small city?"

"They failed to obey orders."

"You are the leader of the mission. It is your job to see that they obey."

"Give me one more chance, General."

"There was an American taken with them. He was not one of ours. Who is he?"

"Unknown. A half-crazed man-beast. A dog delighting in trouble. We found drugs in bags he left near our chairs."

"Just a moment."

General Li Yu put them on hold. He glared at Professor Zhu Sheng, who sat in front of his desk.

"Professor. How close is the boy getting? How serious is the threat right now?"

"It is urgent. He has made a further advance that will lead soon to the proof."

"Explain it quickly to me. In an understandable way. Do not weary me with erudition."

Zhu Sheng cleared his throat.

"If you flip a coin a hundred times, you expect it to land heads half the time. Correct?"

"Of course."

"But it is never precisely one-half. It might be forty-nine times. Or fifty-one times. Do you see?"

"Yes."

"The boy has deduced that the deviation is the square root of the number of tosses. But this was already known. So, if the coin is tossed a million times, the error will be the square root of a million, which is 1,000. Heads will come up somewhere between 499,000 and 501,000 times."

"If it was already known, what has he now done that is original?"

"He has applied this to the distribution of prime numbers, but in a new way. If they are truly random, like a coin flip, any deviation from the appearance of randomness would be very small, in fact the square root of the highest number in that range."

"I do not like erudition. Give me your conclusion."

"Please forgive me. It is this. We know that the expected distribution of prime numbers in any range is the logarithm to the base of a certain complex number, if they are, in fact, random. He is close to proving that that distribution is, in fact, as random as the coin toss. This is what the Riemann Hypothesis predicted. It leads to the cryptography that we presently use."

Li Yu removed the hold.

"Quan Ruxiu."

"Yes, General."

"You may have one more chance. I am sending more men to assist you. You will meet them in Milwaukee. We have learned that the boy is in hiding in the home of his uncle, Joe Weber."

"Shall we take him at that location?"

"No. The cautious wolf fears the snare."

"Then where?"

"Next Saturday they go to a festival in Milwaukee. It is called Bastille Days. We are listening to their phones. They will run in a marathon. You will run with them. And, in the middle of the crowd, you will terminate the boy. And the woman, if she accompanies him."

"Yes, General. We will not fail. It is not possible."

"Good. I am growing weary of failure in Milwaukee. *Bai bai.*"

"*Bai Bai.*"

Chapter Forty-Two

Wayne Hawkin sat silently in Lathrop Willis' office. Willis ran his hands over a soccer ball as they watched a video of a man in a hood speaking in Arabic. The English translation crawled underneath:

"The mujahideen, the lions of Allah and the benefactors of the Ummah, sacrificed their lives for Allah while the Pakistani soldiers spoiled their eternity by giving their lives in defense of the enemies of the Ummah."

Willis turned it off.

"We got thirty of them. Including the man who beheaded the Brit. We lost a few Pakis in the process."

He tossed the ball in the air and caught it.

"You know, Hawkin, I get a chuckle out of the press constantly chirping after a beheading that 'It's not Islam' and 'All Muslims must band together to fight the extremists,' and how we must have an Arab Spring where Sunni and Shiite will suddenly start reading Rousseau and Jefferson and adopt a First Amendment. The truth is, there are only three known methods to contain the undesirable: drones, bribes, and this."

He tossed the ball up again.

"What do you mean?"

"The World Cup. It lets them release a little steam. Have a go at each other. Allows them to stretch their legs a bit other than on the rack. And violence is avoided."

"Are you kidding?"

"I grant you, there's the occasional disemboweling of a referee in Brazil. A goalie shot in Colombia. Thug beatings by the *Clockwork Orange*, Paki-bashing chav element in Britain. But better a referee or a goalie than a world war."

"You're an idealist, Willis."

"Spare me the sarcasm. Let me direct your attention to the Second Punic War. You *have* heard of it, haven't you?"

"I try to forget it. As I recall, your grandfather served, didn't he? I forget his regiment. The Third Agricola?"

"Not in the mood for humor, Hawkin. I'm thinking of the magnificent words of Cato the Elder, nine hundred years before the birth of Islam. *'Cartago delenda est.'* Carthage must be destroyed. But Rome had only one Carthage. We have thousands. From Mogadishu to Damascus. From Lahore to Baghdad."

"We're keeping them in line, by and large. Don't you think?"

"So far. They're divided. They hold each other in check. The eternal balance of the spheres. Sunnis blow up Shiite mosques. Shiites murder Sunnis. We deplore it publicly, and they stay divided."

"For now."

"Can't count on it forever. You know, Hawkin, sometimes at night, in my study, I raise my glass to Cato and say with him 'Carthage must be destroyed.' All of them."

"The Russians and the Chinese would intervene if we tried it. They sit like spiders on the sidelines."

"You're right. The Russian thug? His nickname in the KGB was the Moth. The Moth is flying too close to the flame for his own good."

"He's desperate. Their economy is falling apart."

"And the Chinese thug," Willis said, ignoring the comment. "He's a billionaire. So are his relatives. So long as he can steal, he's content."

"What's the word on Violet Light? Any development?"

"No. Frankly, I'm worried. It's never been mentioned again in anything we've been able to decipher. And, there is one thing in particular that bothers me. We've discovered that the Chinese are building a launch site just over their border with North Korea. It's almost completed. We actually found out about it through our Korean sources. Confirmed by satellite."

"Why would they do that?"

"Don't know. They're not doing it to help the North Koreans. The Chinese understand the psychosis in that country. They know that if the North Koreans launch anything against the United States, the whole mainland of Asia is vulnerable to our weapons. They've actually started to cut off the North from some missile technology."

"So, what are they building?"

"Our people think that they're doing it for themselves. To launch something that they can blame on the North Koreans if it goes badly."

"Such as what?"

"Don't know. Tell me, any update on Milwaukee? Are you still convinced there's a serious threat there?"

"Yes, I am."

Hawkin looked at his phone.

"I've got to answer this. I'll stop by later."

Chapter Forty-Three

"Wayne? It's Audrey."

"What's the latest?"

"I've made progress with the Webers. They get the danger. I called Frannie after I met with them. Joe's girlfriend. She gets it. She'll work on Joe and on Jerry Piano, the policeman friend."

"I have something for you. We interrogated the two men you seized in Madison. You can expect more of them soon. The general in charge of this is getting impatient."

"Who was the American?"

"He was paid to cause trouble at the convention. A red herring. We let him go."

"Wayne, I need more men out here."

"Can't we just put the boy in protection? Pull you out and let him finish his work somewhere secure?"

"I suggested that to Frannie. She doesn't think they'll go for that. For taking Bernie away."

"How many men do you want?"

"A full team."

"Audrey, look. So far, I haven't spoken to Willis about this. But he knows. I'm sure he knows. Nothing goes on here that he doesn't know. There's a statute that plainly states that we can't deploy agents for domestic operations. You violate that yourself. It's much too risky to send a full team."

"Wayne. There's no other way to do this. No one else can do it."

"We already have teams in place. In Manhattan. In Washington. In L.A. and other cities. The Congressional leadership knows. They'd have to publicly object if we were embarrassed in Milwaukee. We're supposed to risk that to protect a kid?"

"Yes. And I want to brief them."

Hawkin was silent.

"Wayne?"

"You'll get your team. When do you need them?"

"This weekend. In Milwaukee."

Chapter Forty-Four

We were standing in a crowd at the starting line on Cathedral Square, corner of Jefferson and Wells, waiting for the Storm the Bastille 5-K Run. Me, Bernie, Terry, Frannie, Trixie, and Jimmy Fieblewicz. Bernie, Trixie and Terry were holding signs that said, "Fieblewicz for Alderman." We planned to walk the route in a group while Jimmy waved and shook hands along the way.

It was the kick-off for Bastille Days, a four-day French festival in the middle of July. Food booths everywhere. Strolling mimes and singers wandered the streets. Musicians played harps, fiddles, accordions, bagpipes, flutes, French horns, and harmonicas. *Chansons populaires* floated along every street in East Town.

There's a fest in Milwaukee every weekend from the beginning of June to the middle of September, most of them on the seventy-five-acre festival grounds on Lake Michigan. Polish Fest, Festa Italiana, German Fest, Irish Fest, Fiesta Mexicana, African World Festival, Pride Fest, Arab Fest, Asian Moon, Labor Fest, Indian Summer. And an eleven-day Summerfest, billed as the world's largest music festival, where bands play on eleven stages all day until midnight.

Bastille Days is the only major fest held downtown on the streets of East Town.

A mime, tall and powerfully built, with a painted-white face and exaggerated red lips extended onto his cheeks, was half a block away. He wore a tight shirt with horizontal black-and-white stripes, and tight pants. Several children giggled as he tiptoed by them and winked.

Suddenly he stopped. He mimed a box and stepped into it. He pretended to try to get out, scratching his head when he couldn't. The children laughed.

"Okay, Bernie, here's the deal. You too, Jimmy."

Trixie pointed down the street.

"There's a lot of drunks out there. Bernie and Terry, you and me are walking beside Jimmy. We hold these signs up. Jimmy, you wave as you walk. Every once in a while, you run to the curb and shake hands. Then run back to us. Got it?"

"Yup."

"Stay away from the drunks. And don't react to anything they shout out. See?"

"Yup."

"Joe and Frannie. You walk alongside Jimmy. Wave. Not a beauty-pageant wave. Do it like you mean it. The crowd has to see a posse. They want muscle."

"Got it."

A block away, Audrey Knapp stood at a booth, eating a cream puff. She was dressed in a peasant skirt and white blouse, with her hair in a bun. She turned to step out into the street when she felt a hand on her shoulder.

"Do not move until I tell you."

She turned to see a Chinese tourist holding a camera. It was pointed at her chest, with his hand behind it.

"What do you want?"

"Walk in the direction of the cathedral. Walk slowly. If you run or turn, you will fall down. I will kneel to assist you. When others come, I will leave to call for help. They will not notice that I disappear. They will also not revive you."

The mime came dancing down the street toward them. Children holding cream puffs stared up at him. He bent down to hand them a flower. Their parents chuckled.

He stopped next to Audrey and the man with the camera. The man froze. The mime shaped a box around them. He lifted a leg to step inside, his hands folded. Audrey shifted slightly to let him in. With his back to the children, the mime unfolded his hands.

The man with the camera fell to the ground, twitching. The mime drew a box around him, and reached in. He held him by the throat and the crotch, and then the mime lifted him high above his head. The man went limp. The mime turned to dance slowly down the street, turning occasionally to pirouette.

The children and their parents clapped.

"Bravo!" said one mother. "Bravo! Bravo! Children, if it's a male performer, you must cry 'Bravo. If it's a woman, you must cry 'Brava.' "

"Yes, Mother."

"Runners on your mark! Get set! Go!"

Audrey ran to the starting line. A few thousand runners and walkers were crowded around Cathedral Square. The serious runners had already taken off. She pushed through the crowd in the back until she saw Bernie and Trixie.

Two more smiling mimes danced into the crowd behind her. They stood nearby, drawing imaginary boxes to strong applause.

The last row of runners took off. The tide was going out. Walkers were next.

"Okay!"

Trixie raised her arm and dropped it.

"Team Jimmy! *Hit the beach*!"

We started to walk down Wells Street, waving at the people seated on the curb and in lawn chairs on the sidewalk. Jimmy ran to the curb about every half block to shake hands and scurry back to us. Trixie and Bernie and Terry raised their signs high. Frannie and I waved to the spectators.

A few of the younger guys who'd had too much beer started to make fun of Jimmy. Some people aren't crazy about seeing politicians campaigning.

"Go back to prison!"

"Get over here and shake hands with the governor!" yelled another.

He pointed at his fly. Jimmy ignored them. He waved and smiled. Trixie poked her sign in the direction of the hecklers.

At the corner of Broadway and Wells, we turned to head down to the Third Ward. A kid in his late teens, blasted out of his mind, came running up to us, holding something. I didn't see what it was until he was almost on Trixie. It was a water gun. He squirted Trixie and ran back into the crowd on the sidewalk. The crowd went wild.

"You bastard! I'll get you," she shouted, wiping her eyes.

But Trixie's a pro. She stumbled on, poking her sign at the crowd.

I noticed two mimes dancing behind us. They were pretty good. They kept pace as we walked.

Ravel's *Bolero* sounded from two large speakers on the sidewalk when we got to the corner of Wisconsin Avenue and Broadway. A Chinese man with a camera was kneeling taking pictures. When we started to cross Wisconsin, he stood up and hurried in our direction, snapping as he came.

One of the mimes danced around us. He suddenly grabbed the man with the camera gracefully, as if he were a ballet dancer holding up a ballerina. He held the man by the throat and crotch, and they danced around in a circle.

The crowed clapped. It looked to me like the mime was crushing the man's throat. The man's eyes bulged, but it must have been an illusion. They were both good actors. The man went limp. The mime danced to the *Bolero* off into the crowd, and down the empty street behind the spectators.

Frannie poked me.

"Joe. I don't like this. Let's get out of here. Get Bernie out of here."

"What? This is fun."

"Are you crazy? That man with the camera wasn't acting. I trust Audrey. We've got to hide Bernie. Now!"

"We'll go home right after this is over."

"I said now!"

I looked up ahead. There were more Chinese men with cameras standing along the route, in front of the people on the curb.

"Okay."

I grabbed Terry.

"What?"

"Terry! Take Bernie and get the hell out of here. Take him to your place. Now."

"What's the matter?"

"Just do it. There's some guys here that are trouble. Do it now."

I grabbed Bernie.

"Bernie, go to Terry's. I don't like what I'm seeing. Frannie and I will take the signs. I'll come get you later."

"Okay, Joe."

Frannie and I took their signs. Terry and Bernie trotted back through the crowd toward Wells. They looked back when they got to Mason Street. The men with the cameras were still walking fast in their direction.

"Pick it up, Bernie! Run!"

They started to trot up to Wells Street. The men ran after them.

"Bernie! Car's too far away! Follow me."

The stained-glass window with Till Eulenspiegel on a donkey below a facade of an Alpine mountain scene was just in front of them.

Bernie and Terry ran into Karl Ratzsch's restaurant.

Chapter Forty-Five

Bernie and Terry stopped as the door closed behind them. The restaurant was half full. Bosco Wallenfang had his back to them as he spoke with a waitress near the coat room.

Two accordions rested on the floor where the quartet usually performed.A sign propped on a chair said: "Quartet on break. Some sharp recorded tunes will be played in their absence."

"Vater Unser im Himmelreich" by the Thomanechor Leipzig floated softly from the speaker.

Terry pushed Bernie toward a staircase in the back to the right.

"They'll be here in a minute. Get upstairs!"

They hurried up an ornate wooden staircase to the second floor. Oil paintings of medieval market scenes hung on either side, with plump, red-faced women selling flowers and jolly men offering fish to passers-by.

They trotted into the second-floor dining room. It was filled with men in dark suits and women in black dresses. The room went silent. A waiter held up his hand.

"I'm sorry, Sir. This is a private party. The Kilbourn Country Club's annual Chaine des Rotisseurs dinner. I'm afraid you must leave."

"We can't," Terry said.

He was shaking.

"Some guys out there are after us."

The waiter raised his eyebrows.

"I'm sure there are, Sir. Even paranoids have enemies. But you must go."

A woman, about seventy, was listening with interest. She was wearing a purple dress and a big hat with two small birds on it.

"They may stay," she said.

The waiter was agitated.

"But Madam. With all respect. This is the Chaine!"

"I know. They may stay. Sit here, Boy."

She motioned Bernie to a seat next to her on the left.

"And you."

She gave a slight wave to Terry Norris and gestured to her right.

"Sit next to me here."

"But Madam von Bierlein! Those seats are reserved for the Master of the Feast! And for the Wine Master!"

She nodded to the waiter.

"We will put them elsewhere. Sit, Boy. What is your name?"

"Bernie Weber, Ma'am."

"A good name. A strong name. And what is your name?"

"Terry Norris."

"Someone's chasing you, are they? How exciting. How low rent. Did you misbehave in some manner?"

"Definitely not."

Waltraud "Wally" von Bierlein was the Queen Mum of Milwaukee, the wealthiest and most influential person in the city. The von Bierleins had dominated Milwaukee industry, banking, philanthropy, and civic affairs for well over a hundred years. Wally's great-grandfather, Augie von Bierlein, had run away from the family tavern in Hamburg when he was seventeen. When he sailed to America as a stowaway on the *SS Katzenjammer*, no one could have known that future generations of Milwaukee's most prominent leaders were being carried across the Atlantic in Augie's historic testicles.

The others in the room nodded approvingly as Bernie and Terry sat down, even though they would have thrown them out the door if Wally hadn't been there. No one in Milwaukee disobeyed Wally von Bierlein.

Downstairs, Bosco Wallenfang saw six Chinese men walk into the restaurant. He picked up menus.

"Reservation?"

"No. We are looking for someone."

"Who?"

"Man and a boy."

"Are they here?"

"Not down here. We must go upstairs."

"It's a private party. Off- limits."

"We wait down here."

"How many?"

"Six."

"Over here."

Wallenfang seated them near the foot of the stairs to the second floor. He distributed the menus.

"May I ask you a personal question?"

A dozen hard eyes stared at him without blinking.

"You are Han?"

The Han of Asia had met their match in Milwaukee.

No one answered.

"But surely not all Han?"

Wallenfang stared at the man to his left.

"I see traces of the Philippines, perhaps? And Borneo?"

One man slowly reached toward his pocket. He stopped, clenching a fist instead.

"Excuse me. It is a subject that interests me."

Bosco Wallenfang took out a pad of paper.

"Your order?"

"We will each have tea. And the check immediately. We may not be here long."

"Very well."

When Wallenfang went into the kitchen, one of the men slipped up the stairs. He hurried back down.

"They are sitting at dinner in a large group. The stairs are the only exit. When they come down, we will follow then."

He pointed to one of the men.

"When they are out of public view, kill them."

The man nodded.

"Our plane will be waiting. You know your travel orders beyond that."

The men nodded.

Bosco Wallenfang returned with a cart. He put a cup and a pot of hot water before each man. A waitress set plates of lemon slices and small pitchers of cream.

"Sugar is on the table," he said. "Your waitress, Marymartha, will bring you the tea selection and the check. I will be back shortly."

Marymartha hurried back into the kitchen to get the teas. Wallenfang headed up the stairs.

"I hope everything is satisfactory?" he asked Wally von Bierlein.

"Perfect. Thank you."

A waiter refilled the water glasses in front of Bernie and Terry.

"Thanks," Terry said. "I'll have the goose shanks, red cabbage, and a Spotted Cow."

The faintest trace of a sneer crossed the waiter's face.

"Sir, this is the Chaine. The menu tonight starts with mushroom soup, and then Royal Ostrea caviar. This is followed by *cochon de lait*, with roasted-sunchoke, leek-vadouvan marmalade sauce. We finish with Araguani chocolate mille-feuille."

"Got it. Can I get a brewski, though?"

"Sir, wine is available. In this case, an excellent Henri Jayer Richebourg Grand Cru and a Domaine de la Romanee-Conti."

"Thanks. I'll have the red."

"Do you speak French?" Wally said.

Terry bowed his head.

"Oui."

"*Assistez -vous aux diners Chaine de Rotisseur dans d'autres villes quand vous faites des voyages d'affaires?*" ("Do you attend Chaine dinners in other cities when you are traveling on business?")

Terry bowed again.

"Jacques Cousteau. Escargot. Ways and means."

"*Quelle genre de betise est-ce?*" ("What kind of nonsense is that?")

He nodded.

"Joaquin Andujar!"

"Pass the bread, please."

Wally selected a piece of bread. She tasted the soup.

"It is divine!"

She tugged on the waiter's sleeve. He was a kid from Milwaukee Area Technical College, studying to be a chef.

"Young man, you must throw yourself upon my fork to spare me further harm!"

Startled, he grabbed her spoon. She swatted his hand.

"My fork, I said. Not my spoon."

An older waiter, a Riverwest stoner with a fringe of grey hair around a large bald spot, looked closer at Norris.

"El Wingador!"

Terry tried to shush him. The man snapped to attention. He went instant Berghoff waiter, erect, slightly supercilious, no eye contact with the customer. But it was too late.

"Why did he call you that?" said Wally.

"There was this wings-eating contest at this bar?" Terry mumbled. "The Uptowner? I won it."

"How many did you eat?"

He stared at Wally's wrists.

"I can eat some wings."

"Attention, please!"

A man stood up and gently rapped on a glass.

"Can I have your attention."

Terry's phone vibrated. He looked down at the text:

Where the hell are you?

Terry thumbed back.

Second floor, Karl Ratzsch's. Chinese downstairs. Get here. Bring Jerry.

"I am Trevor Williams," the man said. "I am the Master of the Feast."

He paused for polite applause.

"You will hear from several others. I give you the Wine Master, Ben Carter. Ben?"

Carter stood to more light clapping. A medal the size of a salad plate hung around his neck.

"What's the medal?" Terry whispered to Wally.

"Because he's the Wine Master."

"How much did he drink?"

"A hogshead. Pay attention."

"I also give you Ted Wallace, the Master of the Sweets. He and Ben are also my fellow officers of the Kilbourn Country Club."

Wallace also stood. All three bowed to the diners and to each other.

Each of the men from the Kilbourn Country Club wore a tux and white shirt but no tie. Dominated from infancy by prominent parents, they existed their entire lives in emotional straitjackets. Their solitary act of defiance, their sole display of wormlike insouciance, was to refuse to wear a tie. The light from their eyes looked as if it had come from a dead star five billion years ago. A whiff of formaldehyde accompanied them.

"Let me explain a brief history of the Chaine," Williams said, fully aware of the skeptical glances from the diners and the rumors about him and his admission to the Kilbourn Country Club. Yes, he had established Aryan descent through each of his four grandparents. But it was whispered that his documents hadn't been reviewed by experts. They'd been approved by his golf buddy on the selection committee! And without the required report from DYNA-GENE!

Williams was a Milwaukee banker, that is to say a pigeon who made occasional trips to Wall Street to have his feathers plucked. He would tour the derivative-poisoning, aluminum-shuffling Wall Street fraud nests, escorted down the hall by thin, fraud-on-the-hoof young men with radioactive eyes. They would eye the plump butterball from Milwaukee, grin, and whisper to each other behind his back. "Can we do derivatives again? No, too soon. Too risky."

A manly chap, Williams had played JV Hockey at Country Day and touch football at Colgate. He wanted to hedge!

"Hedge?"

They chuckled

"We'll hedge your hungry ass! Five percent of your portfolio. And leverage? There you go! Another two percent. And what about volatility? There, Sir, three percent more! The investment? Oh, that! Korean and Chinese illiquids. Bursting with value, Sir! Thinly traded so you buy at a discount."

He would then return to Milwaukee for a proper round of burping and boasting in the clubs before his feathers grew back and he was summoned back to Wall Street.

"And finally," Williams said, "the roots of the modern Chaine go back to France in 1248 under King Louis the Ninth. It was originally the Guild of the Goose Roasters. Tonight, we are all goose roasters. Let the feast begin! Bon appetit."

Terry looked at his phone.

"Piano on the way. Stand by."

Bosco Wallenfang emerged once again from the hallway as Williams sat down.

"I am the maitre d', Bosco Wallenfang. Is everything satisfactory?" he said.

"Quite," said Williams.

"Not entirely," said a man with an English accent who sat beside him. Born Jack Stubb in Manchester, in Milwaukee he called himself Bosworth Field. Bosworth had been selected for page service in the House of Lords at the age of sixteen but escaped at the train station in London and made his way to the United States. He was a thin man, with filmy eyes and wispy hair combed onto his forehead.

"Bacchus is thirsty!" he said. "We are denied the treasures of the grape! Wolfgang to the rescue!"

He waved an empty glass.

The English are generally well regarded in the City of Milwaukee, where people think that Sean Connery and Crocodile Dundee are English. And even more so in the suburbs and the clubs, which suffer the Sudan of prestige droughts. People are desperate. Their distended egos and hollow eyes demand relief. In the Englishman, they find it. Viewed as an itinerant mendicant, prized for his accent, he sends pleasing prestige signals wafting through the room just by saying "Good morning."

The more accomplished English adventurers and remittance men end up in New York or L.A. after they're smoked out in Europe. The rest migrate to the Midwest, where they can make a tidy living off of their accents.

We even accepted a famous criminal. The Brinks bank robber managed to live in a Milwaukee suburb for twenty years until the cops came to get him.

Wallenfang scowled.

"The Wine Master will order the wine."

The Englishman held his empty glass on his head.

"Wolfscat! A whiff of the grape! *Verstehen sie? Verdun, verstehen*! Wolfie to horse!"

"We take our orders from the Wine Master. It will be served shortly."

"You may wonder about the origin of my name," Williams said to Bosworth Field, who had been staying at the Kilbourn Country Club for several months in return for wittily insulting club members at arts fundraisers.

"But enough about me. What do you think of me?"

"What?"

"Just joking. Carry on."

"We stood with William the Conqueror at the Battle of Hastings. We were Will's Men."

"Stout lads, the Williams," said Bosworth. "I'll wager they were archers at Agincourt too!"

"That, too."

"Wielded a sword for the Tudors, no doubt? And not above using the dagger, eh?"

He pretended to thrust up from beneath the table.

"Very likely."

"Patriots, the Williams. Patriots all!"

Williams reddened at the compliment. He nodded as he sipped his wine.

Wally von Bierlein didn't conceal her irritation as she contemplated Williams and his crew. She shrugged and reached for her glass.

Norris felt his phone vibrate. He pulled it out.

Chapter Forty-Six

Jerry Piano and I stood inside the front door of Karl Ratzsch's. Officer E.R. "Ernie" Doggs, one of Jerry's buddies, was with us.

A quartet was playing.

Ich bin ein musikante, und komm aus schwabenland . . .

Bosco Wallenfang came hurrying up to us.

"Fang!"

"The Pianoman! Table for three?"

Jerry looked at the six Chinese men sitting at the foot of the stairs.

"Not this time. I need to talk with you, Fang. Can we go in the kitchen?"

"Sure."

"See those six guys?"

"Yeah?"

"See their check and the cash on it?"

"Yeah."

"Go get it and meet me in the kitchen."

"Okay."

Ernie and I stood at the door. Jerry came back five minutes later.

"Joe, when I give the word, get Terry and Bernie down here. Ernie, when they come down, take them in the squad and get out of here."

"Right."

Wallenfang came out of the kitchen.

"There's a problem," he informed the table.

"What?" said the man who had placed the order.

"The money you gave us is counterfeit. We are investigating now."

"That is not possible."

Jerry and Ernie walked over to the table.

"What's happened?" Jerry said.

"Counterfeit money," Wallenfang said. "These gentlemen will have to stay here while we resolve this."

"Must be mistake. We have no knowledge. Here is other money."

"Too late," said Jerry. "You all have to stay here."

"I stay. The others leave."

Ernie Doggs moved closer to the table.

"No one leaves," he said.

Wallenfang disappeared back into the kitchen.

"Must speak to manager," the man said.

The quartet had finished the song. Fred walked over to join them. He pushed his Alpine hat back slightly.

"What's the matter?"

"Counterfeit money," Jerry said. "We're checking into it now."

The skin on the leader's face tightened. He placed a one-hundred-dollar bill on the table.

"We have diplomatic immunity. This is discrimination. Hostile environment. Need to leave."

It was easy to tell that Fred had a glass eye. It was the one with the tear in it. Fred stared at the man.

"We will obey the police. You must stay."

Jerry pulled out his walkie-talkie and nodded at me. I hit my phone. Terry Norris looked at the text.

Get down ASAP! Go to squad in street. Now!

The Master of the Sweets was speaking.

"The history of the sweet dessert is fascinating," Ted Wallace said. "The Romans ate an onion for dessert. Sweet desserts only came into favor nine hundred years ago."

Wallace was an internist who had suffered financial reverses. His shiny tux looked scandalously like a rental. Just as gazelles are the

McDonald's of the Serengeti for lions, doctors are the McDonald's for brokers.

The broker says, "What's that, Doctor? You fly your own plane? That you built yourself from a kit? Beyond belief! And I thought Jefferson was a Renaissance man! And you put syrup on your pancakes? That you drain yourself from trees in Vermont on land you own? Well done! Now, I have an investment that might interest you, Doctor. Subordinated, tax-advantaged, mezzanine put securities. Confidentially, Sir, it's called STAMPS. We only have a few, but I might be able to get someone of your stature a tranche. Perhaps five hundred thousand dollars? What? A million? Oh, Doctor, I don't know, but I will try. I surely will try. Thank you, Doctor! And next week we may offer a few swaptions! Very confidential. I'll get back to you."

Doctors are the only professionals who love jargon from other professions and presume to lecture others using it, even practitioners of the other professions. Wallace started to go deep into the history and theory of the Araguani chocolate mille-feuille.

"We have to go," Terry whispered to Wally. "Sorry to run."

"I'll go with you," said Wally. "I'm tired of these *couillons* (assholes*)*."

Wallace paused as Wally von Bierlien rose to leave. Williams looked agitated at the departure of the Queen Mum.

"Surely you will stay for the meal, Madam von Bierlein?"

"Not this time, Mr. Williams. I am indisposed."

They watched her disappear into the hallway along with the two freeloaders who'd bolted in from the street to defile their dinner.

I saw Terry and Bernie hurry down into the main dining room behind an elegant woman wearing a hat with birds on it. The Chinese men started to get up. Jerry Piano put his hand on his gun. He stepped up to the table.

"Sit down. If you try to leave, we will arrest you."

The men sat down. As the woman walked by the table, she turned suddenly to put a hand on one of their shoulders.

"I want you to know that I simply *adore* your Colonel Chow's Chicken. It's a guilty pleasure of mine."

She smiled graciously at them as she swept past followed by Terry and Bernie. Officer E.R. "Ernie" Doggs hurried after them

Outside, the street seemed to be full of mimes, dressed in black-and-white shirts and black trousers. Two sat in a white truck that said "Prime Movers" on the side. Several dozen more roamed the sidewalk. Others performed across the street, attracting the attention of the few pedestrians who weren't watching the Run for the Bastille.

"How lovely!" said Wally, clapping softly. "So many handsome young mimes! It's like a blaze of monarch butterflies clustering on a bush! Bravo! Bravo!"

She shook hands with Terry and hugged Bernie. As she turned to walk up the street, they hopped in the squad with Ernie Doggs.

Chapter Forty-Seven

General Li Yu stood at attention before the desk of Yan Shifan, who looked at him for several minutes before telling him to sit down. The general sat erect in the chair and said nothing.

"I have lost patience with you," Shifan said.

"Yes, Sir."

"You have heard nothing from the men you sent to Milwaukee?"

"No, Sir."

"A team from our special forces goes to Milwaukee to terminate a boy and disappears?"

"Our last communication was before they entered a restaurant. The boy and the uncle's friend ran in. Our team went in after them. Then, communication ceased."

"The cooks and the waitresses killed them?"

"I apologize, Sir. We lost two of our men before that. It was a festival. Some enemy assets were in the crowd."

"Then, how did we lose the rest of them?"

"I don't know."

Yan Shifan turned to a TV on the credenza behind him.

"They found out about the launch site in North Korea. We had the Koreans take responsibility, but some television stations in the United State are raising questions about our involvement. We are starting to get requests for clarification. Here is my response that will be broadcast tonight."

Yan Shifan appeared on the screen. He was seated at his desk. Two Chinese flags flanked him. A reporter in her thirties, with a pad and pencil on her lap, was asking him questions.

"And for my next question, Sir, a small number of television stations in the United States have falsely implied that some construction activity by our neighbors in North Korea is the fault of the Chinese people. Could you comment, please?"

Yan Shifan nodded on the screen.

"It is a slanderous farce by blind fools and idiots bereft of every elementary ability to discern the truth. No matter how hooligans and rogues under the guise of TV producers may work to falsify the reality, they can never hide the truth."

The reporter nodded vigorously.

"It is as I suspected."

Yan Shifan turned off the TV.

"Words of admonition are bitter, but they must be said. And understood. I am dissatisfied with your performance. You have one more chance."

"Thank you! Thank you!"

"If the boy succeeds, the Americans will discover the purpose of the launch site."

"He will not succeed!"

"Describe what you have called the Vancouver option. What does it entail?"

"It has been changed."

"How has it changed?"

"We had planned to seize him. But now, that presents unacceptable risk."

"What will you do now?"

"We will send a plane with twenty-five men to Vancouver. Our best men. We have effective access to the city as we please."

"And then?"

"From there, they will fly on commercial flights to San Francisco. They will have identification showing them as businessmen and students. In San Francisco, they will board a private jet leased by one of our agents in Silicon Valley. When it lands in Milwaukee, it will receive no notice."

"And then?"

"They will disperse and enter the city individually. It will be impossible to track them all. They will have all necessary information on the boy's location, and the locations of his friends and family. They will terminate him."

"And the withdrawal strategy?"

"Some will fly to San Francisco from Chicago. Some from Milwaukee. When they get to San Francisco, they will fly individually back to China."

Yan Shifan was silent.

"It cannot possibly fail."

"No plan is incapable of failure. I approve what you say. But also this: if you fail, you will never have another chance."

"Thank you!"

"You may leave."

Yan Shifan watched the general leave. A young girl in a silk teddy slipped into his office, carrying bottles of massage oil. He waved her away and picked up the phone when she was gone.

"Hello."

"Commence the planning for a human flesh search."

"Yes, Sir."

"It must be confidential. Share no names until I give you the order. Do not activate it until I call you personally. Understood?"

"Understood, Sir. But confidentially, may I know the identity of the subject? It is needed to plan the search."

"General Li Yu."

Chapter Forty-Eight

Audrey Knapp looked down at the flashing red light on her phone and dialed.

"What's happened?"

"Audrey," Hawkin said, "I have to order you home. Immediately."

"Why?"

"Willis found out. The House Intelligence Committee found out."

"Found out what?"

"What you're doing out there. The Committee got a Freedom of Information Act request on you. The Chinese ginned it up out of California."

"Don't answer. We're exempt from FOIA."

"Of course we won't. But the Committee's going El Niño on us. Afraid the press will find our other domestic ops. Someone on the committee called a hearing. They subpoenaed me and Willis."

"Public hearing?"

"No. Of course not. Nonpublic, with no written agenda. But I'm not going to perjure myself. Lamar has it worked out that they won't ask names and locations. Willis and I can handle it so far. But direct orders from Willis. Come home."

"I can't."

"That's an order, Audrey. We're not risking our mosque surveillance to protect one kid."

"Wayne?"

"Yes?"

"I'll obey the order when I'm working. But do one thing for me."

"What?"

"I have vacation saved up."

"How much?"

"Twelve weeks. I request permission to take that now."

"Where are you going?"

"None of your business."

"Who are you going to be with?"

"None of your business."

"What are you going to do on vacation?"

"None of your business."

"Okay. It's none of my business. Can I tell Willis that you're standing down?"

"You can tell him I'm on vacation."

"That's what I'll tell him. And by the way, no more mimes are coming to Milwaukee. Understand?"

"I understand."

Chapter Forty-Nine

A black Lincoln stopped in a driveway next to the Longworth House Office Building.

"What's the matter?" Willis said to the driver.

"Demonstrators. They stake out the witness entrances. They probably think you're testifying on the drone thing."

"Can't they be arrested?"

"Courts said they can stand here as long as they don't go near the building."

Willis slumped back in his seat.

"Damn. We should have gone in as tourists. Like we usually do. But I hate the lines."

Hawkin looked out the one-way mirror that served as a side rear window.

"There are a lot of them."

The driver started to nudge the car through the crowd. Some people shouted. A small band of counterdemonstrators shouted back.

"Stop the bombing!"

"Libtards!"

"Repukes!"

"Demo *rats*!"

"Teabillies!"

Hawkin unwisely lowered a window slightly to look straight into the face of a woman with stringy hair and pointed glasses.

"You hierarchical, monotheistic, European fuck!" she screamed into the car.

Hawkin winced as he closed the window.

"No drones!"

"Moonbats!"

"Talibangelicals!"

"When the mob gets a fever, best to let it run its course."

Willis looked at several note cards.

"You set on your testimony?"

"All set. No questions on names or locations. Right?"

"Right. Lamar's got it in hand."

The driver kept pushing slowly until he got beyond the crowd. He pulled up alongside a door in the middle of the building. A guard opened their door and Willis and Hawkin hurried into the building.

"Where's the hearing?"

"Longworth 1334. We'll meet Lamar's staff there. They'll get us set up."

A woman in her twenties greeted them at the door of the conference room. She wore a blue blazer, white blouse, and red plaid skirt.

"I'm Yolanda Molica."

They shook hands.

"I'm on the Chairman's staff. I'll escort you to your chairs. Some of the members are here already. The Chairman will start the hearing when the others get here."

The room had chairs for about sixty spectators. They were empty. A few members had taken their seats facing the witness chairs and were skimming through notes. Molica took Willis and Hawkin to two chairs in the front, beneath the raised area where the Congressmen faced them. Several more members walked in. One of them sat down in the middle. He waved at Willis.

"That's Lamar."

Hawkin nodded.

There were twenty members of the Committee. The Chairman called for attention when the last member was seated. The few staff in the room left and closed the doors.

"I am Congressman Lamar Patterson, Chairman of this committee. We have a very important task today. This hearing is closed to the public. It has not been disclosed on the House schedule. There is no staff present. No transcript will be made. We are conducting this because we received a Freedom of Information Request on alleged operations by our intelligence agencies within the United States."

He sipped from a glass of water.

"We will not respond to it. Indeed, the FBI informs us that it may have originated from our foreign adversaries. However, several members of this committee requested that we conduct this hearing. They note that the CIA is prohibited by statute from conducting domestic operations. I have full confidence in our agency and am confident that they will answer in a manner that satisfies this committee."

He sipped again.

"Mr. Willis, do you or Mr. Hawkin wish to make a statement?"

"No, Sir."

"Very good. We'll open the hearing to questions."

A Congresswoman on the Republican side raised her hand. She was gorgeous, her beauty marred only by a pair of wild, blazing eyes, like a pair of AIM-9 Sidewinders coming at Mach two straight down your throat. The Republicans were pushing her as a consensus VP candidate to fight the war on women thing. This was a chance to get her some foreign policy chops. She locked in on Lathrop Willis.

"Sir, as an American and a mom, I am concerned about domestic drones. Why are you droning Americans?"

"The short answer is that we're not," Willis said. "We're prohibited by law from doing that."

He was barely courteous.

It's that aqua buddha from Kentucky who's feeding this crap to his disciples. Try discipling on some other freak.

"Sir," she said.

She looked down at a sheet of paper in front of her, which said, "United Concerned Citizens" at the top, followed by a P.O. box number. Underneath that, two paragraphs: Positive: Values, freedom, guardians, liberty, defense, jobs, American, morning, industry. Mix for us! Negative: Taxes, bloated, controls, debt, quotas, crime. Mix for them!"

"Let me tell you what I stand for," she said. "Our values are the guardians of our liberty. Taxation is the enemy of industry. But industry is the source of our liberty."

"Pardon me?" said Willis.

"It is vital to keep American values in the forefront of our kids' freedom! But our opponents want to use tax controls to bloat debt quotas!"

"I beg your pardon," said Willis. "I'd be happy to answer a question."

She grew anxious.

"Our opponents believe in taxing government crime-quotas! But I believe in the defense of jobs and American morning values!"

The Chairman raised his hand.

"My distinguished colleague makes excellent points, but I think I'll rule at this point that we've gone a little astray from our agenda. Congresswoman, I invite you to direct a question to Mr. Willis."

"Okay. What right do we have to use the drones at all? Anywhere?"

The Chairman put his hand on his chin.

What's with the drones? The goddamned drones are down the hall! In another hearing.

"The Second Amendment, Madame Congresswoman. The agency has a Second Amendment right to use drones in our defense."

"Got it. Thank you."

The Chairman held up his hand again.

"I'd like to gently remind the panel that this isn't the drone thing. That's another committee down the hall. This is the domestic-ops thing. And let me pose a question to Mr. Willis. For reasons of national security, we won't mention names or places in connection with any operation. Can you assure us that the CIA is not conducting any operations within the United States?"

"We are forbidden by law from doing so, Mr. Chairman. The agency has not ordered any of its agents to conduct operations in the United States."

"They're all volunteers? Just kidding."

"Good one, Mr. Chairman. Very good."

"Thank you. Mr. Hawkin, do you have anything to add to Mr. Willis' testimony?"

"I agree with Mr. Willis."

"Very good. Very good."

The Chairman turned to the panel member.

"Any other questions?"

A member on the Democratic side raised his hand. He had a square jaw, perfectly combed hair, and slightly dimpled cheeks.

"Mr. Willis, as a hypothetical matter, what would you do if you believed there was an urgent need for you to intervene in an American city, yet you were prohibited from doing so?"

"I would inform the FBI, turn over our information to them, and request that they take action."

"Excellent. Thank you. It's just that we got a FOIA request for information in Milwaukee . . ."

"Out of order," said the Chairman. "I'm afraid that's out of order. I set up ground rules that were supported by a majority of this committee in advance of this hearing. We won't use names or locations."

"Thank you. I have no further questions."

"Are there any other questions of our witnesses?" the Chairman said. He paused.

"Hearing none, we will excuse our witnesses and adjourn. Thank you, gentlemen."

Willis and Hawkin walked by themselves down the hall toward the exit.

"Milwaukee's off limits, Hawkin," said Willis. "I want to be perfectly clear about that."

"I understand."

"I know Audrey. She's smart and she's tough, and she has a conscience. But it's time to get our priorities straight."

"Right. But you know the threat to the kid is real. The chatter is getting stronger. Our plant in their leader's office says they're sending men and a plane to get him."

"That's hard for me to believe. They can't really think that the kid can solve that problem. But if they do come, let the FBI handle it."

"They can't act as fast as we can. Too many layers. They're already stretched too thin. They claim they need more proof before they can get involved."

"We've had this discussion before. Go to the police. I'm getting tired of this."

"They don't know what to do."

"We can only get involved if it goes overseas. I repeat, I'm not willing to risk what we're doing in New York and L.A. for this."

"Then, who will protect the kid?"

"Milwaukee. And whatever raggedy militia they can scare up."

"Then God have mercy on his soul."

Chapter Fifty

Jerry Piano sat down for lunch at Polonez, a popular Polish restaurant on Milwaukee's south side. A pretty girl with braided blond hair poured him a glass of water. She wore a white blouse, embroidered vest, full skirt, and apron.

"Lunch, Jerry?"

"Yeah. I'll have the Polski talerz."

"Bottle of Okocim?"

"Nope. On duty. I'll take a Sharps."

"Anyone joining you?"

"One."

She went back into the kitchen.

Audrey walked into the restaurant. She sat down in the booth facing Jerry.

"Thanks for being here."

"You don't have to thank me," Jerry said. "I just want to know something. What are you after?"

The waitress reappeared to put a bottle of Sharps and a sausage sampler on the table.

"Would you like to order?"

"No thanks," said Audrey. "Water's fine for me."

"Okay."

She took a pitcher from a tray and poured. Audrey waited for her to leave.

"I'm not after anything. I talked to Trixie. And to Joe. Did they fill you in?"

"Yeah. What's really going on? What do you want?"

"We have information that the Chinese government is sending a plane to Milwaukee. We don't know when, but soon. It's coming from San Francisco. It'll have a lot of men on it. They'll try to kidnap Bernie Weber. Or kill him. I want you to deliver fifty Milwaukee police officers to the airport when I tell you."

"Is that all?"

Jerry chuckled.

"You know, you really are a piece of work. What's your name?"

"Audrey Knapp. Did you call the number I gave Trixie?"

"Sure. And it backed you up. Only problem is, I didn't know who I was calling or where it was."

"Did you check it out?"

"Sure. And it doesn't exist. It's the only number we've never been able to trace."

"That should tell you something. Look, Milwaukee is a little oasis in a bad world. I'm not kidding. If you do nothing, Bernie's going to disappear."

"Get the FBI."

"They passed. Too busy. Too rigid."

"How about your own kind? You're not that rigid, apparently. You roam around and do whatever you guys want."

"You're right. Ordinarily. But they canceled this operation. Too much heat on it. Political heat."

"Then, why are you here?"

"I'm on vacation. I'm on my own. I don't back down. I don't walk away."

Jerry snarfed down a sausage and swigged from the bottle.

"I can't get fifty guys. The chief would have to sign off on it. He's strictly by the book. He isn't gonna buy into this bullshit."

"Can you get anybody?"

"My squad partner. Ernie."

"How about state militia?"

"National Guard. It takes the governor to call them out. He's weak. He'd do it if he could pose for holy pictures with the Guard after they arrested them, and perp walked them around the Capitol. He's an expert at disappearing when anything goes down."

Jerry threw two tens and a five on the table. He stood up.

"Can't you do anything?" Audrey said. "I know Milwaukee doesn't have a militia."

"You're wrong."

He wrote a phone number on a napkin.

"This is my cell. Give me twenty-four hours' notice before they land."

"I already have your cell."

"I thought you might."

He turned to the door.

"Where are you going?"

"The Milwaukee militia. I'm going to get them."

Chapter Fifty-One

Two men entered a small conference room in the Milwaukee County Courthouse. One wore a wrinkled sport jacket and blue jeans. The other had on a blue suit and red tie. The man in the tie closed the door.

"All right, James."

The man in the suit motioned to the other man to take a seat.

"We're gonna kick some knowledge over the situation."

James sat down.

"How'd I get you, anyway?"

"I'm free, man. To you, I'm free. Court appointed me."

"I thought you was disbarred."

"I'm back. Just a little weed. They let me back in."

"Man, how'd I get you?"

"I can leave. I can leave right now."

The lawyer stood up.

"You on your own?"

"No, that's all right. Stick around."

"So, James. Here's the thing. This is some serious shit. They got you on three felonies. Fraudulent bills to the state for the day-care piece."

"I don't know nothing about it."

"You didn't even own the day-care center, am I right? It was your girlfriend?"

"Right. It was her. She said, 'sign these things.' And I did."

"How long were you dating her?"

"Six months. We was getting close."

"So why'd you sign the bills?"

"Help her out. I bogod the situation. But they a dead cat on the line."

"I got some ideas," the lawyer said.

"What?"

"First thing, we got the bad optics to overcome."

"What?"

"The sign over the day care center door. It says, 'The tooth fairy don't leave loose change.' Judge isn't going to like that."

"It's not my sign. I didn't put it there."

"Right. So, here's the thing. Today we plead not guilty. I work on the DA. But we got a secret weapon."

"What?"

The lawyer pulled out a newspaper clipping. It showed a picture of a man with a rubber smile and reptilian eyes. James winced.

"Man. Them some hard eyes."

"Bankster. He sold some crooked stocks. Made a billion dollars. Threw a lot of brothers out of work."

"So?"

"DA kicking the legals. Then the man go 'I don't admit or deny it. But I won't do it again.' "

"*What?*"

"It's a white-man thang. Judge threw it out. The man walked."

"What?"

"Listen to me. We got plenty to work with here. Now let's go in. Court's starting."

James and his lawyer left the conference room. They walked into the courtroom of Judge Frawley Watkins. There was only one spectator inside, Jerry Piano, who sat on a bench in the back.

The prosecutor was already seated at the front table. James and his lawyer had barely sat down at the rear table when the door to the judge's chambers opened. A bailiff, clerk, and court reporter walked into the courtroom, followed by the judge.

"All rise."

Everyone stood.

"Please be seated."

Judge Frawley Watkins adjusted his robe as he sat down. He cocked his head sideways, appearing to look at them with one eye.

"Call the first case."

"State versus James Parsons," said the clerk. "Appearances, please."

"Assistant DA Timothy McGuckin for the State of Wisconsin, Your Honor."

"Attorney Antonio Holmes for the defendant, Your Honor. And let the record show that the defendant, James Parsons, appears in court with me."

"All right. Be seated. We're here to enter a plea by Mr. Parsons. Mr. Parsons, you are charged with three counts of submitting false claims to the State of Wisconsin for payment of day care services to indigent children. How do you plead?"

"How do I plead?"

Jimmy shook a little.

"Yes. How do you plead?"

"Won't do it again! No, Sir. Don't admit it or deny it."

"*What*?"

"No!"

Holmes was on his feet.

"No! He pleads not guilty!"

"Is that right, Mr. Parsons?"

"Yes! Yes!"

"Very well. We'll set the case for trial in ninety days. See my clerk when we adjourn and agree on dates for trial and pretrial motions. We'll send them in an order. Anything else?"

"No, Sir."

"No, Judge."

"All right. We are adjourned."

"All rise," said the bailiff.

Frawley Watkins slipped back through the door into his chambers. Holmes and McGuckin took out their iPhones and whispered around the clerk. James sat silently at the table.

"I'll call you," Holmes said to Parsons as he hurried past. "Tomorrow."

He left the courtroom, with McGuckin right behind him.

"James!"

Parsons looked around. Jerry Piano walked up to the table.

"I want to talk with you in the conference room."

"I gots a lawyer. I ain't sayin' nothin'."

"It's not about this. I can help you on this. I need something."

They walked back to the conference room. Piano closed the door.

"James, I'm going to tell you something. This case is wrong. It was your girlfriend, right?"

"I ain't sayin'."

"I know it was her. Not you. I'm going to tell the DA. I think we can get this kicked."

James still said nothing.

"But I need your help."

"What?"

"Your nephew. Dartanian Cheese. I need to speak with him. Tomorrow at eight in the morning. At Miss Polly's Diner on North. You know it?"

"Yeah."

"I need to see him there. And you with him."

"We ain't comin'. He didn't do nothin'. I ain't speakin' to you."

"I got some word for you. You can go to prison for ten years and deal with some punk-ass wannabees every day. Or you can meet me for breakfast tomorrow with Cheese. I won't ask you about your case. I won't ask him what he's been up to. Which is plenty. I will help him. And you. But I need him to do something for me."

"What?"

"You'll find out tomorrow. At Miss Polly's."

"What if I don't come?"

"Your sorry ass is toast."

"What if he don't come?"

"His sorry ass is burned toast."

"What you want? I ain't comin'. And I ain't bringin' him there."

"James."

Piano leaned forward in his chair.

"There was a time you stood up. Remember? Long time ago? You were one of Father Groppi's commandos. The older guys at MPD remember you."

James didn't reply.

"You marched with Father Groppi over the Sixteenth Street Bridge into a screaming mob. For open housing. It took a lot of guts. The crowd on the other side cursed you."

"I remember."

"Bottles were thrown. Some people got seriously hurt. You got hit on the head."

"I remember."

"You stood up for something. And now, there's a chance to stand up again. Our country has enemies. You can help."

"Didn't do no good. They still be hatin' on me."

"I'm not. Listen to me. I need your nephew and his friends to help me. Some very bad people are coming to Milwaukee. I need help."

"You ain't going to arrest him?"

"No. You have my word. I need his help."

Piano got up.

"See you tomorrow at eight. At Miss Polly's."

James sat in silence as Piano left.

Chapter Fifty-Two

Miss Polly and her sister tidied the table they'd set after the officer called. Miss Polly looked at the menus one last time. All prices had been scratched out with two-dollar increases written on the side. "Bacon and Eggs" now said "$7.95." The old "$5.95" was crossed off. Folks from downtown were coming to Thirty-Fifth and North.

Jerry Piano and Ernie Doggs walked into the restaurant. Miss Polly hurried over to greet them.

"Here's your table. Would you like coffee?"

"Yes. Two coffees. Thanks."

They sat down. The door opened. James Parsons walked in, with two men close behind. One was in his early twenties. He wore a baseball cap with a Baltimore Ravens logo, tilted forty-five degrees to the right. His tee shirt had a picture of Benjamin Franklin from the one-hundred-dollar bill. Franklin wore a pirate kerchief and one earring. The other man was older. He was about six feet six inches tall, with a bodybuilder's chest and arms. He looked as if he could have pancake-blocked an NFL lineman. His head was completely shaved.

The three sat down with Piano and Doggs. James pointed to the younger man.

"This my nephew. Mr. Dartanian Cheese. And this his friend. Ulysses."

Ulysses offered no last name. None was requested. After the cordials, they ordered. Miss Polly refilled their coffee cups.

"Dartanian. I'm going to be blunt."

Jerry Piano put down his cup.

"I need your help. I need you to do something."

Cheese shook his head.

"I ain't sayin' nothin'. Not about me. And not about no one else."

"I'm not asking you to. What I need is different. Very soon a plane is going to land at Mitchell Field. It will have men from China on it. They want to hurt or kidnap a Milwaukee boy."

Cheese frowned.

Po-leece pullin' some Asian shit. Krew dogs ain't doin that! We ain't one eight seven nobody. Big foe need to lay it down fo me. Po-leece layin' in the cut waitin' fo yo ass.

"Do it yoself."

"I would. But I can't get enough officers. Here's what I need you to do. I need you to take your Two-Seven krew and go down there when I give the word. I want no weapons. You will stop them from leaving the airport. You will restrain them. I will have a couple of guys from MPD with me. We will arrest them."

"Man. We be fightin', we be arrested. We ain't doin' it."

"Don't rule it out. Listen to me. We are forming the Milwaukee Militia. It will be one regiment with four battalions. You will be the colonel in command of the regiment. When I leave you, I'm going to see the Three-Five krew."

"What? They fake-ass, gangsta wannabees. Ain't havin' nothin' to do with the Three-Five."

"We need eighty men. Twenty from the Two-Seven. Twenty from the Three-Five. Twenty from the Serpents. And twenty from the Jacks."

"Serpents? Jacks? No way. They bad, man."

"They think highly of you, too. I'm not leaving here 'til you say yes. We're suspending Operation Krew Kut. You are Colonel Cheese, commanding officer of the Milwaukee Militia."

"Ain't doin' it, man."

Piano touched his phone.

"Listen to this."

"Walkin down Two-Seven with two Glocks strapped. Biskits and shellz goin' off like a new Eyeraq. Gonna put a lick on the weed man."

Piano stopped the recording.

"You recognize that voice?"

"You got a warrant, man?"

"I get a warrant when I want a warrant. Operation Krew Kut gets a whole lot of warrants. So, you put a lick on the weed man? And you were in possession?"

Dartanian Cheese kept quiet.

"There's enough on you and your krew to put you in Waupun for a long time. A very long time. When you get out you, will be aged cheddar."

Piano stopped for a response, but Cheese still kept quiet.

"We're not walking away from violent crimes," Piano said. "We will hit the krew for rapes. And murder. And armed robbery. But the weed man was not hurt. And he is still a weed man. The DA will stand down on other things."

"How you know?"

"I talked with him. If you assist the police, he will not go after stolen cars. He will not go after weed. He will not go after felony possession."

Cheese said nothing.

"Your uncle helped this city when he took on a mob. He did the right thing. What do you say?"

"Thoughts are present."

"Dartanian."

James Parsons looked down at the table.

"Do it."

Cheese said nothing. Ulysses looked straight ahead without expression. They sat for a long time.

"I do it," Cheese finally said.

Piano nodded.

"We need you to win this."

"I go yard."

"Can I count on you?"

"God be my secret witness."

Cheese touched two fingers to his lips.

"Word is bond."

Chapter Fifty-Three

Jerry Piano and Ernie Doggs walked into Azteca on Oklahoma Avenue. Signs on the wall said "Gallego for County Board." They sat at a table with two men.

"You are Hector Gallego?"

"Yes."

Gallego wore a floral shirt, untucked. His hair was neatly combed.

"And, this is a friend of yours?"

"He is my campaign manager."

The two men chuckled.

"He is Fulgencio."

"Let me tell you why I called you. I need your help."

Gallego nodded gravely.

"In a short time, a plane of Chinese soldiers will land at Mitchell Field. They have come to kidnap or kill a boy in Milwaukee. We have formed a militia to meet them. Four battalions of twenty men each. The Jacks will provide twenty men. You will command them."

Hector Gallego nodded again. He tried not to laugh.

The president wants you to play golf with him and Tiger Woods this Saturday. Miss America is coming over in half an hour to spend the night. And the Pope wants to make you a cardinal. These cops. They continually bust my balls.

"I see. And what is my rank? How much will I be paid?"

"A major commands a battalion. You will be paid jack. It is a service you owe to the city."

Gallego shot him a feline smile.

"Can't do it, man. I'm running for the County Board."

He pointed to the signs.

"You are? What's your platform?"

"Jobs for at-risk youth. I am for jobs and the youth. The children are our future."

"Is that right? I have some advice. If you want jobs, don't shoot the hiring manager of the city's biggest company."

Gallego's face tightened. He didn't reply.

"Someone robbed the hiring manager for the company. He was having dinner in this neighborhood. When he went to his car, two men pulled guns on him. Have you heard?"

Gallego still didn't reply.

"He hit the alarm on his key chain to get help. They shot him. A bullet went into his brain. They killed him."

"Serpents did it."

"Serpents say Jack did it."

"They lie."

"The investigation is going on. We will find who did it and send him away for life. We will not ease up on violent crime."

Hector and Fulgencio sat very still.

"But we searched your house. We found some interesting things. Guns. Weed."

"Search warrant, man. You got one?"

"We went in by permission."

"Who? No one there, man."

"There was a gentleman on the sidewalk. I said, 'Can I go in this house?' He was cooperative. He said yes."

"A drunk on the sidewalk? You scare the shit out of him. Who was he?"

"I didn't catch his name. But it doesn't matter. Guns and weed don't interest me. Not with you. Not if you help the MPD."

"Who else is in it?"

"The Serpents will have a battalion of twenty men. I've met with Nestor Maldonado."

"Man! Serpents no good. *Hijos de puta!*"

"You will have an alliance for one day. You will fight together to help the city."

"Who else?"

"The Two-Seven krew. And the Three-Five."

"Bad. They got a very bad reputation."

"They're not alone. You in or out?"

"What happens if I don't do it?"

"You'll find out."

"I was afraid of that."

"You in?"

"I'm in."

They shook hands.

"Major Gallego, I'll call you very soon."

Chapter Fifty-Four

Audrey Knapp's phone vibrated. She looked down at the text.

Proved it. Meet you at Bavette? Third Ward? Two today?

It came from Bernie Weber's phone. She texted back.

Yes. Two today.

She walked into the restaurant at one-thirty. A waiter showed her to a table.

"Thanks, but I'd like that one in the back corner."

"Okay. I'm Ed. I'll be your waiter."

He seated her in the corner.

"Will anyone join you?"

"Yes. One. I think."

Ed put down two menus.

"I think I'll just have coffee."

"Thank you."

Audrey slipped out of her chair when Ed left. She walked into the men's room. It was empty. She walked into the women's room. It was empty, too. She examined the door in the rear. It locked from the inside.

She returned to her table and looked around. It was a small restaurant, with ten tables and a dozen stools at the counter. It was almost full. She examined the diners. They were all couples or groups of women, mostly young, deep in conversation. She sipped her coffee.

Bernie Weber walked in a little after two. She waved to him. He walked over and sat down.

"Hi," he said, shyly.

"Hi, Bernie. Are you alone? Anyone outside?"

"Nope."

"Good."

She sat back and took another sip.

"Thanks for texting."

"Yeah. I'm sorry I ran away from you in Madison. I didn't know who you were."

"That's okay. You were smart. You're smart to run away until you know who's helping you."

"I know you guys want the proof I've been working on."

He took a flash drive out of his pocket and handed it to her. Audrey looked at it before zipping it in a pocket inside her jacket.

"That's incredible. How'd you do it?"

"I like this stuff. I suddenly had an idea."

"What?"

"I read that it's been proven that the first six billion zeroes obey the Riemann Hypothesis. They stayed on the line. So, I got computer time at the UW. But there were some close calls. Zero number 17,144 came right down on the line."

"But it didn't break through?"

"It didn't break through. But it was a close call. I realized that I could keep using computer time and go up and up, but I could never be sure there wasn't a higher number where it violated the hypothesis."

"Then what?"

"I could prove that an infinite number of zeroes stayed on the line. And I could prove that *every* number up to an unknown number n stayed on the line. So, I just had to prove that n itself was infinite. That there was no number that broke the line."

"Just? That's all?"

"Yeah. So that's what's on that drive."

"Bernie, you are terrific! You are wonderful!"

Audrey squeezed his hand.

"Could you talk to some of my guys back at my office? Like right now?"

"Right now? You mean here?"

"You got it. Right here!"

Audrey pulled out her phone.

"Hello?"

"Wayne? Audrey. Get Gieck on the line!"

"What? Now?"

"Yes, now. I'm sitting here with Bernie Weber. I have a flash drive with the proof in my pocket. I want him to describe it to Maynard."

"Are you kidding?"

"No."

"Are you secure?"

"Yes."

"Hold on."

She heard it ring.

"Maynard? This is Wayne. Audrey's on the line."

"Yeah?"

"Maynard. I'm putting Bernie on the line. He solved it. I have it on a flash drive. I want him to give you an overview."

She handed the phone to Bernie.

"This is Bernie. What? Yeah."

He listened.

"Yeah. So, the numbers bounce pretty close to the line. I could show that every number up to n stayed on the line. I had to prove that n is infinite. No number breaks the line."

He listened again.

"How? It's really like proving that the prime numbers themselves are infinite. But in a different way."

Bernie continued to whisper into the phone. He finally handed it back to Audrey.

"Get the drive home immediately," Hawkin said. "I'll have a courier to you in two hours. At the airport. Look for the text."

"Right. And I need something, Wayne."

"What?"

"We're monitoring flight plans from San Francisco to Milwaukee. There's a plan filed for a flight in seven days. The plane is owned by someone you and I know. He is under surveillance for stealing corporate trade secrets for the people in question."

"Yes?"

"Send two planes. One for the courier. And one to stay here for transport."

"For transporting what?"

"The people coming from San Francisco."

"I can't do that, Audrey. You know my orders."

"I know them. I'm not asking for men to engage on the ground. I'm asking for pilots and a few baggage handlers to load and secure men who need loading and securing. Men you will want to question."

"How the hell are you going to get them without a team to help you?"

"I have a team. A Milwaukee team. Look. I'm an agent on vacation who needs transportation. That doesn't contradict what Willis wants."

"I'll send a plane. For transportation only."

"Right."

"And you are with the FBI. Is that clear?"

"Of course."

Audrey put a ten-dollar bill on the table and stood up.

"Bernie, I've got to go. "

She hugged him when he stood up.

"You are a wonderful young man. A truly talented young man. Thank you."

She put her arm in his.

"Could you walk me to my car?"

Chapter Fifty-Five

Six Chinese officers in uniform sat around a conference table. A seventh man sat with them. He wore a mauve beizi, a cloak, and a teal jinguo, a scarf looped around his neck, in the fashion of a Ming-dynasty concubine. He was completely bald, with a hairless chin, arms, and legs, and had fake eyebrows lined in with rust-colored lipstick.

"We will now hear from Tuzi Diao," said General Li Yu. "Comrade Diao will brief us on his most interesting hypothesis. As background, you will recall that we have monitored the phones of some of the Weber boy's protectors for some time, including the police officer, Piano, who has had discussions of interest. He appears to have some general idea of our upcoming visit to Milwaukee. Some of the language used is ambiguous. Comrade Diao has proposed an interpretation for us. Comrade Diao."

"Thank you."

Diao stood up and fussed with his scarf.

"I know some of you. As further background, I hold doctorates from Nanjing University in English and philology. I have an interest in deciphering messages from foreign intelligence agencies. In the service of China. In the service of the Han nation."

He peered around the table. No one said anything.

"I bring an urgent message from my father. Today, the American Secretary of State is visiting South Korea. He is a wolf with a hideous lantern jaw. We don't know why he is traveling to South Korea to plot with his Korean puppets. The question is, why of all the days of the year, as numerous as the hairs of a cow, did he choose to come now? A week before our launch in North Korea?"

He paused, as if he were waiting for questions. None were offered.

"The American president always goes reckless in words and deeds, like a monkey in a tropical forest. Their chief running dog in South Korea is a prostitute. She is a rotten banana. A guide dog for the blind. A plague."

Several men nodded. Diao turned to click on a power point. Two men whispered urgently when his back was turned.

"He is the leader's adopted son."

"Yes."

"Is he competent?"

"Do not ask."

"Is his science legitimate?"

"Do not ask. The leader's judgment should not be questioned. Nor his son's."

They stopped when Diao turned around.

"This is the policeman. Jerry Piano. A guilt-ridden ape, capable of murder."

Diao pointed to the screen.

"A rough sort. Massive and brutish. Potentially violent. I will now play some of what Piano recorded on his phone. "

He clicked on an arrow.

"Walkin' down Two-Seven with two Glocks strapped. Biskits and shellz goin' off like a new Eyeraq. Gonna put a lick on the weed man."

He clicked on another arrow.

"Lay it down fo me. Here the foe one-one. We the folks. They packin' chitlins. We ain't hattin' up. Esseys, they betta come correct with some respect."

Diao clicked off the recording.

"This obviously contains a coded message. The Americans use their minorities when they want to confuse the enemy. They used Navajo Indians in the Second World War to deceive the Japanese. But they will not fool us. Piano has talked to men using the code names Hector, Nestor, Ulysses and Dartanian."

Diao snickered.

"Three of these are names from the *Iliad*, an epic poem in early European history. Another is a French swordsman in the seventeenth century. They are trying to trick us. Piano is trying to get their help. We hear him say that the police won't help. And our complaint to their Congress removed their agency. But in discussing Ulysses, the man labeled Dartanian said this."

Diao clicked again.

"We need mo' round-the-way dogs. Like Ulysses. Dog be draped. Dog a diesel."

Diao stopped the recording.

"Dog a diesel," Diao repeated. "The man is obviously not a dog, whoever he is. It is an insult. And a diesel is an engine, not a man."

He looked around for approval.

"My professional opinion is that we have misinterpreted this phrase. It is not 'dog a diesel.' It is 'dogged easel.' "

He looked around triumphantly. No one smiled. One officer raised his hand.

"But he mentions dogs earlier. A draped dog and a round-the-way dog."

"To throw us off the scent."

"What does that mean? What does it mean to say someone is a dogged easel?"

Diao nodded.

"We assume from the conversations that Piano will convince a few undesirable elements to meet our men when they arrive, perhaps to protest. I believe that the artist who drew this picture will be one of them."

He showed a mural of several African American men holding their hands to the sky, with necks bigger than their heads, and unusually large eyeballs.

"There is a street artist in Milwaukee named Hole Money," Diao said. "This is known to us from our agents who are embedded as students in Milwaukee Community College. Hole Money is a struggle artist who paints revolutionary themes."

"Where does he paint them?" said an officer.

"On people's garages and fences. On buildings. The city is his easel. His signature is a pitchfork with three tines. He is persistent. His work is everywhere. My thesis is that Ulysses is Dogged Easel. And Dogged Easel is Hole Money!"

He paused to let his discovery sink in.

"Excuse me, Comrade, but even if he is, so what? What should we do with this information?"

Diao nodded vigorously.

"It is unlikely that our team will meet anyone. Piano is one man with no resources. It is almost certain that our men will arrive and leave without detection. But if a few undesirable elements do show up, the leader of our team should engage Hole Money in discussion. To express solidarity with the struggle in the American streets. The rest of the team will slip away to do their duty."

"Excellent! Most insightful!"

General Li Yu clapped as he walked over to Diao to hustle him out the door.

"We owe you a great debt for this insight, Comrade. And now, we will discuss certain routine military matters that will not interest you. But we will put your wise insights to good use."

Diao bowed to light applause and was hurried out the door.

"We have heard from the leader through his son," said the general. "It is of high importance that we terminate the boy now."

"How do we know the Americans have not decoded our plan already?

The general shook his head.

"We salt our messages with false information. The Americans would have no choice if they read it. They would have to respond to certain things. But there has been no evidence of heightened surveillance anywhere in the world."

"If undesirable elements meet our plane, what are our orders to respond?"

"It will be at most a handful of urchins. Their natural resentments make them ripe for recruitment by a few of our men. The rest of our team will deploy."

"But what is our response if it is the police? Or members from their agency?"

"It will not be. Piano revealed that there will be no police. And our man's complaint to their Congress bore fruit. Their agency has withdrawn."

"We are ready to deploy."

"Do not fail."

Chapter Fifty-Six

Wayne Hawkin answered his phone.

"Get in here, quick. I just spoke with Maynard Gieck."

Lathrop Willis was on the phone when Hawkin hurried into his office.

"Lamar. Now, I'm telling you. You've got to take it out."

He listened.

"What? I don't care what they say in the White House. Call the Secretary of Defense. Call the Joint Chiefs. *Take the goddamned thing out*!"

He listened again.

"It's not an attack on China. That's why they're launching it from North Korea. They'll save face. Strong disapproval in the United Nations, etcetera, etcetera. But not technically an attack on them. What? Okay. Call me back."

He glared at Hawkin as he hung up.

"Gieck read Weber's proof. It scans. It's obvious now how they used it to encrypt. At least it's obvious to Gieck. And the NSA."

"Did you run their messages?"

"We started with messages just before they built the launching site. They're set to launch their own kinetic bombardment system in forty-eight hours. Violet Light is their Sif. Jade Rabbit was their recon launch. Once they land it on the moon, we can't touch it."

"Can't we jam it? Remotely?"

"Possible. I don't know. But what if we can't?"

"Then bomb it on the moon."

"Might not be able to. I don't know if we have the tech to pinpoint it. Even our friends in Congress aren't going to support bombing a Chinese moon site in front of seven billion spectators."

"What did you tell Lamar?"

"I said take the launch site out. Before the launch. It's technically in North Korea. Not an affront to China. They'll file a grievance. But North Korea has no credibility. All their other neighbors will thank us."

"What did Lamar say?"

"He's on it. Push back from the White House. But we can't have this. We can't let China plant an unreachable weapon system that can destroy us."

Willis pointed to a folder.

"IBM just sold a Chinese company the blueprints of its high-end servers and the software that runs on them. The man who supervised the cybersecurity of China's strategic-missile arsenal works for the company. He publicly stated that they're developing a full supply chain of computers and software on top of IBM's technology."

"Isn't it illegal to sell that to them?"

"Not if you get permission. IBM got permission from our government to do it!"

"What?"

"I'm getting tired of this, Hawkin. Our major companies are all multinationals. They only care about meeting projections. Other people are giving up their U.S. citizenship to dodge taxes. But if a war breaks out, they'll show up mighty quick as tourists in Naples and Aspen. I'm tired of this!"

His phone rang again.

"Lamar? What?"

He listened.

"Lamar, you tell them real blunt. They take this thing out or I'll drop in men to do it by hand! What? I know it's illegal. *They'll be volunteers*!"

He slammed the phone.

"There are still a few patriots left, Hawkin. You and me. And the people in our agency. And Lamar. He may still get it done."

Willis pressed a remote.

"The war has shifted to tech. Look at this."

The first slide said, "People's Liberation Army Unit 61398—China."

A description of its key personnel followed.

"They're dedicated to hacking into our government, industrial, and banking networks. Now they'll have IBM equipment to do it."

Willis clicked through more slides. Syrian Electronic Army, APT 28-Russia, and slides on Tunisia, Thailand, Iran, and ISIS. Each showed key personnel.He turned it off.

"So far, we've blocked them. We can drone some of them when we have to. But not in Russia and China. Or Thailand."

Willis took the stopper out of the decanter.

"Sherry? Pretend we're back in happier times."

He poured two glasses and handed one to Hawkin.

Chapter Fifty-Seven

The private jet started to descend when it crossed from Iowa into southern Wisconsin.

"We're beginning our descent into Milwaukee. Thirty-five minutes to landing," announced the pilot."

Chen Ping stood up to face his men.

"What we do, we do for the future of China. We are Han. We are the only civilized race. Our culture is the oldest in the world."

The men were quiet. He made eye contact with several of them.

"We do not fail. We are the Han, the Yan Huang Zisun, the descendants of Yan and Huang. We are Huaxia, the civilized people."

Several men nodded.

"America is a country of mixed race. They are *cha de*, the inferior race. Their military are thirsty beasts who have drenched the world in blood."

More nods.

"To be turned into iron, the metal must be strong!" one man shouted.

"Stop a gun with your chest!" shouted another.

"We will perform noble feats to wipe out our enemy!" a third man said.

"I will repeat our instructions for the last time," Ping said. "When we land in Milwaukee, the plane will proceed directly into the hangar of Bullion Aviation. There will be a bus waiting outside. It will take us to our staging area."

"Where is that?" said a man in the front.

"A house near the airport. We have embedded men in Milwaukee to gather industrial information. One of them rents a house close by. You will deploy from there."

Ping paused.

"You have been provided with maps of the city and all necessary addresses for Bernie Weber; his uncle, Joe Weber; police officer Piano; and the address for family friend, Terry Norris. You will deploy in four teams. Are there any questions about the operational plan?"

There were none.

"Any questions about transportation out of Milwaukee? You have been given your itineraries. Is there any doubt about how you will get to your designated airport?"

Several men shook their heads.

"Your weapons will be delivered to the house. You will have no weapons on you if you are stopped for any reason on the way from the airport. And if possible, use no weapons when you dispose of the boy."

The men nodded. They sat back as the plane continued its descent.

Chapter Fifty-Eight

A crowd of black and Latino men, most of them young, slouched in the parking lot of Bullion Aviation. They looked at the two police officers and the woman who were talking at the edge of the lot.

"There's a bus on the side," Audrey said. "It has two men in it."

Piano nodded.

"Ernie will arrest them. Ernie!"

"No."

Audrey put her hand on Ernie Doggs's arm.

"I have two men and a plane on a side runway. For transportation. They'll do it."

She took out her phone.

"Bus is around the corner. Two men. Secure them for transport."

"Good," Piano said. "I'll get these guys ready to go."

"Okay. I'll clear the intake area. They have no flight activity for the next two hours. We'll clear the personnel inside."

"How do you do that?"

"The FBI asked the airport to delay all private flight plans for two hours into and out of Bullion after the San Francisco flight."

"Okay."

Piano walked over to the front of the crowd.

"Attention. Line up. Jacks on the left. Then the Two-Seven. Then the Serpents. Then the Three-Five on the right."

The men rolled slowly into position, making elaborate detours around each other.

"All right. First of all, none of you has a weapon, right? Of any kind."

Some nodded.

"Okay. Let me put it to you bluntly. Some people have bad memories. It happens. I am going to wand each of you now. If you have a weapon, I will take it, and you will leave the formation and be subject to arrest."

There was total quiet.

"You have five minutes to go back to your cars before I check you. To have a cigarette maybe. To refresh your memories. To stow gear. Back in five."

Most of the guys hurried to their cars. Piano went into Bullion's office. Audrey was inside.

"So, Rob," she said to a man behind a desk. "This is Officer Doggs of MPD. He's assisting the FBI. How many people are here now?"

"Me and my secretary."

"How many will meet the plane and guide it in?"

"Into the hangar? Two guys."

"Okay. Law enforcement has secured this area. You and your secretary must leave here immediately. Go to the main terminal and wait for me to call you."

"Do you want my cell?"

"I have your cell."

"It's unlisted."

"I know. And before you go, tell your two guys. The minute the plane is in the hangar and the passengers start to file into the office area, they must leave. Understand?"

"I understand."

"They must turn and exit out the hangar door, not into the office. Don't touch the baggage. Understand?"

"I understand."

"If they fail to leave immediately, and interfere in the office, they will be arrested. Understand?"

"I understand."

She looked at the clock.

"The San Francisco flight should land in twenty minutes. Have you gotten any deviation from the control tower?"

"No. Twenty minutes is about right."

"Good. Tell your men, and then leave with your secretary."

"I will."

The three of them went back out to the parking lot. Most of the crowd had reassembled. A few stragglers ambled into formation.

"All right," Piano said. "Members of the Milwaukee Militia. *Attention*! Stand straight!"

A few men stood straight. Most shifted a little. Others simply looked at him.

"A plane will land in twenty minutes. It will have about twenty Chinese gentlemen on board. They are here to hurt Milwaukee. You will restrain them."

No one said anything. Most stared at him, looking for the scam.

"The order of battle is this. Three battalions stand in the front. Colonel Cheese and Ulysses will lead the Two-Seven to face the enemy in the middle when they come from the hangar into the reception area.

"Major Lavarnay Jonikin and the Three-Five will make a stand on the right flank. Major Jonikin. Who is your gunny?"

"What?"

"Who is your sergeant?"

"Pimpmaster Charles."

He pointed to a tall, thin man in sunglasses with an exceptionally prominent Adam's apple. The man wore a lime-colored, three-piece suit with an ivory tie and a coral shirt. His hat was a deep raspberry. He chewed on a toothpick. An equally tall woman held his arm. She was pretty, dressed in shorts and a tight blouse. The thin man held up his hand.

"I am not a pimp. I clean the pimps off of Three-Five. Here I am known as Charles."

"Very well. But who is the lady?"

"The lady is Miss Feline Fox. My assistant."

"This may not be the right time for the lady."

"Any time the right time for Feline Fox."

"Very well. Major Nestor Maldonado, who is your gunny?"

"El Capirucho."

He pointed to a small man with twinkly eyes. The man flashed his grills to show a variety of metal teeth. Largely gold or silver, with an occasional diamond.

"Very well. You and the Serpents will stand on the left. The Serpents and the Three-Five will prevent an end around. Like a kickoff team. The runner can't be allowed to get outside."

Many of the men nodded.

"Major Hector Gallego, who is your gunny?"

"Fulgencio."

"Very well. You and the Jacks will circle around the building and observe them get off the plane. When the last man from the plane is headed into the reception area, the Jacks will engage from behind. They'll attack the enemy from the rear. Major Gallego, send four men onto the plane and restrain the pilots too. The FBI informs us that they are part of their team."

Ulysses raised his hand.

"What we do with all of them?"

"Bull rush them. Throw them on the ground. Hold them until they're taken away. Officer Doggs and I cannot intervene. But if they commit a crime in our presence, we will respond."

Ernie Doggs ran his fingers over his billy club and his taser.

"How many of you served in the military?" said Piano.

Ten men raised their hands.

"Where did you serve?"

The men laughed.

"Hey, Mister Taliban, talley me banana," one of them sang.

"Okay. Good. Any questions?"

The man who sang raised his hand.

"Is this, like, legal?"

"Yep. Doctrine of exigent circumstances."

"Aha."

"Who the lady?"

"FBI," Audrey said. "We really appreciate working with the Milwaukee Militia."

Chapter Fifty-Nine

The plane from San Francisco rolled to a stop inside the hangar of Bullion Aviation, a small, private facility on an isolated edge of the private aviation sector of Mitchell Field. The two men who signaled it in chocked the wheels and helped with the door and steps. They hurried out the hangar door after the steps were secured.

Twenty Jacks circled in front of them. The two men froze. Hector Gallego stared them down.

"You with the Chinese, man?"

"No! *No!*"

"Get out of here, man."

The men trotted away. The Jacks waited. When the last passenger walked through the door into the reception area, the Jacks swarmed into the hangar. Four of them in durags scrambled up the steps into the plane to get the pilots. The rest ran toward the reception area as shouts and screams came from inside the plane.

Chin Ping stopped abruptly as he came through the door to reception. He looked at the mob. Ulysses stepped forward and stood in his face.

"I am Ulysses."

"You are Ho Money!"

In the fourteen years that Ulysses had spent at Green Bay Correctional, not a single prisoner or guard found it prudent to call him anything but "Sir." Not even a light insult such as "asshole," and certainly not Hole Money or Ho Money or anything else.

"You callin' me Ho Money?"

The thunder started to roll.

"Ho money? Ah likes mah fish wet and slippery!"

Ulysses leaped on Ping, squashing him to the floor.

"Werd 2 da motha!" shouted Dartanian Cheese. "Dis yo boy DC krew daddy! Step to me fo a serious beat down!"

The thunder of eighty men screaming carried out to the street as they charged Ping's men. A few of them turned to run back into the hangar. A swarm of Jacks smashed them back onto the heap of thrashing bodies.

The battle cries of the battalions exploded through the room.

"*La puta que te pario*!"

"Jumpstreet*!*"

"*Carajo*!"

"We the folks!"

And in Mandarin. "*Jibai! Erbi! Shabi!*"

The Chinese fought back. Clusters of men rolled out from the pile. Jontaveous Deeks of the Three-Five was down in a corner. Deeks, head highly domed, eyes the size of two hard-boiled eggs, just as smart as the businessmen who made him sing Christmas carols at the annual scholarship dinner until they heard he represented with the Three-Five krew. Deeks, son of Sergeant Lamont Deeks, who had won a purple heart and bronze star in Vietnam, had always wanted to give back. Deeks did just that now, as his hands tightened around the throat of Ch'en Cheng-Hui, son of Gansu provincial official, Ch'en Kuan, Kuan the Thief, knifed by a desperate peasant when Kuan stole his land.

Lavarnay Jonikin was in trouble nearby. Jingguo Kang of Heilongjiang Province had kicked him in the groin and chopped him in the throat. As Kang drew back his hand one last time, Pimp Master Charles gave him a running kick in the head. Charles, the star of the North Division High School soccer team until he was arrested for borrowing a car without permission from the owner. Before he was expelled, he had once free kicked so hard it had broken a goalie's shoulder. Kang tumbled onto his side and rolled away screaming as he clutched his head.

When Charles turned around, with sunglasses and toothpick in place, he was smashed onto the ground by Chonglin Tao of Guandong Province. Tao the Pervert, as he was called in grade school, and Tao the Burglar in high school. Tao kicked Charles in the side and head and drew up his foot to smash his face.

But Feline Fox brought in the artillery. Her job was to approach the enemies of Pimp Master Charles from behind and deliver an ostrich kick between their legs. And at this she excelled.

As Chonglin Tao raised his foot, Feline Fox caught him squarely on target. Tao collapsed with a groan, to fight no more that day.

Across the room, Lupe Peligro of the Serpents was barely conscious, taking mortal leather from Feng "Jiba" Dai of Anhui Province. Feng Dai had a twisted, brutal face with an unusually thick skull and cheekbones. Dai the Animal, as he was known and feared in Anhui Province, had joined the special forces in return for pardons for the rapes of peasant girls.

Lupe was a man of violent countenance, known on the streets of Milwaukee's south side as El Feo. You would move away if you saw him on a bus. But next to Dai the Animal, Lupe looked like George Clooney.

The Animal made the mistake of lifting his leg for one last kick, not seeing Feline Fox running toward him. Feline Fox kicked Feng Dai on the run squarely in the boiler room. Dai fell writhing on the ground.

Jerry Piano stood in the rear. He tased the few Ping men who managed to break through. He threw them, spasming, back into the crowed to see them disappear under the crush of bodies.

Swinging his billy club, Ernie Doggs jumped in and out of the pile. He saw El Capirucho unconscious on the ground. The man standing over Capirucho held a blackjack. Doggs hit the man in the back of the head. It sounded like the meat of Babe Ruth's bat hitting a fastball.

Audrey Knapp stood near the door, talking on the phone. One of Ping's men broke free, stumbling toward her. She drew and tased him. He fell back and was dragged into the pile.

The door out into the hangar opened. Two tall men wearing FBI ball caps ran into the room. They each dragged one of Ping's men from the heap, gave him an injection, and dragged him by the heels out into the hangar. Then, they returned to do it again.

"The men on the bus," Audrey said. "And the pilots?"

"All secured and on our plane."

They injected and dragged two more men out into the hangar.

The fight was beginning to die down. Ping's troops were either unconscious or held down by clusters of men.

Jerry Piano blew a whistle. The fighting stopped.

"Keep holding your man down until we remove him. Well done, men. Well done, Colonel Cheese, Major Jonikin, Major Gallego, Major Maldonado. Well done, gunnies. *Well done!*"

At that moment, the door to the outside opened and *Milwaukee Journal* reporter Roland Cheek entered the room.

Chapter Sixty

Cheek took in the scene. Two men in FBI caps dragging out limp bodies. A mob sitting on the floor, many bleeding or holding their heads.

He slid up to Jerry Piano.

"Heard there was noise in here. Something going on, Officer?"

"Who are you?"

"Roland Cheek of *The Milwaukee Journal*. Transportation reporter."

He handed Piano a card. Piano looked at it.

"It says 'Political Reporter.' "

"Sorry, wrong card."

Cheek reached into his other pocket and handed Piano another card. It said, 'Roland Cheek, Transportation Reporter.' "

"What's going on, Officer?"

Piano put his arm around Cheek's shoulders and turned him around.

"Routine disaster drill, Roland. Students. Ten dollars an hour. Ketchup. That sort of thing. But I have a tip for you, Roland. Really big. Potentially explosive."

Cheek took out his pad.

"What is it?"

"There's a house on Bolivar Street, near the airport. It has a fence that's six inches over code."

"Address?"

"2913 South Bolivar."

Cheek wrote it down.

"And what's big about it?"

"It was just built. And no one knows who owns it! They keep to themselves. Neighbors saw a woman in a burka in the backyard. The men who come by have beards. And two of them wear turbans."

Cheek scratched some more notes.

"What else?"

"Surface-to-air missiles, Roland. I don't have to tell you the danger. So close to the target. The neighbors can't see into the backyard."

"Are any missing?"

"The FBI is checking. But they could bring them in a pickup truck. We're talking a possible search warrant. Joint FBI and MPD situation."

Cheek's eyes got shiny.

"When?"

"Don't know. Shall we say, maybe soon. Maybe very, very soon."

Cheek stuffed his notepad into his jacket and turned toward the door. Piano put his hand on Roland's shoulder as he walked him out.

"You got to level with me, Roland. You find out something, you got to drop a dime. Give me the four-one-one."

"Maybe. We'll see."

Cheek smirked as he hurried out the door.

Chapter Sixty-One

In the middle of the Yale campus, on College Street in New Haven, sits a white, wooden building with a small, manicured lawn. Its only identification is a small sign with brass letters, difficult to read unless you're standing at the front door. The sign says, "Elizabethan Club."

Its vaults hold the first four Shakespeare Folios; one of three known copies of the 1604 Hamlet; a letter from Queen Elizabeth to Lady Southwick; a medal celebrating the defeat of the Spanish Armada; and a lock of Byron's hair. Cole Porter, a member of the Lizzie, mentions the Club in two of his songs.

Hawkin and Willis sat on slate-blue, leather chairs in the drawing room. The door was closed. A large oil painting of Queen Elizabeth in ruffled collar and curious Tudor headpiece kept watch over the room. A brass plaque under the painting said, "The Virgine Queene."

A plate of scones lay on a table between the men, with two pots of honey and butter. A pot of tea, two cups, a silver pitcher of cream, and a silver bowl of sugar sat next to the scones. A decanter of sherry with two glasses sat on another table nearby.

"We did it," Willis said. "We launched from the George Washington. Privately told the Chinese and the North Koreans to stand down. Violet Light is destroyed."

He pushed a remote, lighting a screen in the corner. A woman holding a microphone was speaking, her hair blowing in a stiff breeze.

"David, I'm standing here in Seoul. It's been three hours since the U.S. attack on North Korea. The people in Seoul are on edge. They're afraid of war."

"What can you tell us about the attack, Lindsay? Was it a nuclear site? The White House won't comment."

"Don't know at this point. There was no known nuclear activity there. The speculation here is that it was a demonstration to tone down North Korea's nuclear development. Stop the threats or Pyongyang is next."

"And what about the Chinese? It was close to their border."

"The Chinese certainly aren't happy, David. A spokesman for the Chinese Embassy in Seoul expressed what he called 'deep concern' about what he referred to as 'an attack on a sovereign nation.'"

"But, of course, it wasn't their territory, so they weren't directly confronted."

"Right, David."

"And, what do you hear about the knife attack on the U.S. Ambassador in Seoul? What is the latest on his condition?"

"He has superficial wounds. He's resting in the hospital. The man who attacked him is in custody. No word yet on whether it was in retaliation for the bombing, but . . ."

"Wait. Sorry to interrupt you, Lindsay, but the North Korean spokesperson is speaking live. We go there now."

A stocky North Korean woman in a military uniform stood at a lectern. She spoke in English.

"The United States is a big country and it bombed our research park investigating cures for childhood disease, not knowing shame like children playing tag. With its large physical size and oblivious to shame of playing hide-and-seek as children with runny noses would has bombed our research facility. The bombings by agents of the U.S. imperialist aggressors show that they are cannibals and homicides seeking pleasure in slaughter."

She turned to a new page of notes.

"And today, a patriot attacked the U.S. Ambassador to the entity in the south. The knife slashes of justice were a deserved punishment on war maniac United States. Martyrs severed their fingers to throw at him. Martyrs self-immolated and threw bodily fluids on him."

Willis chuckled. He turned it off.

"All baloney. One nut attacked our man and failed."

He poured two glasses of sherry and handed one to Hawkin.

"To Cato. Violet Light *delenda est!*"

"To Cato."

They drank.

"But how did you pull it off?" Hawkin said.

"End run. The president wouldn't do it. Lamar and the Chairman of the Joint Chiefs pushed it. The president delegated it to the Defense Secretary, and he did the right thing."

Willis handed his phone to Hawkin.

"And you've got to see this. They took out General Li Yu. Human flesh search."

A news anchor in Beijing read from a script, while English subtitles crawled underneath.

"Li Yu, the once-celebrated general who because of corruption lost both fortune and honor, ended his pathetic and shameful life on a sickbed under supervision. He accepted a huge number of bribes. An anti-corruption team sent by the leader to his opulent, three-thousand-square-meter mansion in Beijing discovered a mountain of cash, jewels, paintings, and antiques. There were also prostitutes."

She looked up for emphasis.

"His next of kin have not claimed the body."

Willis took back his phone. He chuckled again as he poured more sherry.

"Too marvelous! Too magnificent! What do we do to deserve such bounty? Violet Light and Li Yu on the same day. Another one out of the way."

"What about the boy? Have you talked to him?"

"I talked to Bernie. I talked to his uncle Joe. The boy's shy. He won't work for us."

"He's really helped us."

"He has a brilliant future. Who knows? May have to chase him again."

Willis raised his glass.

"And to Audrey. She did splendid work. She obeyed us the way we obey Congress. Thank God."

"To Audrey."

"*Pocula elevate. Nunc est bibendum.*"

"*Bibemus.*"

Chapter Sixty-Two

"Today's Election Day."

Trixie said it more in reflection than as a statement of fact.

"I hate election days."

Audrey and Trixie sat at a table in Serb Hall. It was three-thirty in the afternoon. They each drank coffee in the lounge.

Serb Hall is ground zero for all political activity in Milwaukee. Labor Unions hold their monthly meetings there, along with most candidates holding fundraisers. Presidential candidates speak at Serb Hall. Candidates jockey a year in advance to hold their election night return parties here.

Serb Hall's twelve bowling alleys were the set for the *Bowling with the Champs* television series. There is no vault at Serb Hall. But if there were, it would hold a bowling ball autographed by Earl Anthony, one of Liberace's jackets, and a few strands of Bob Uecker's hair.

Trixie had gotten the jump on Flores' handlers. She'd reserved the ballroom for Jimmy Fieblewicz's victory party before they even tried.

"I wanted to say good-bye to everyone," Audrey said. "I'll kind of miss them."

"Glad you're here."

"Shouldn't you get back in there? Check on the GOTV? Phone banks?"

"I'm tired. They know what to do. I got a bad feeling about this one. Usually I go on staff for a while when my guy wins. This one I'm not so sure."

"You can always get a new candidate."

"I can't stand newbies. They say too much. A beat-up old hound like Jimmy is easy to handle, but they don't win. They make people tired."

"Trixie, you ever been in love?"

"One time. Once. I fell for him when I was twenty-two. He strung me along. He was the sun for me. And then one day the sun didn't rise. I was thirty-nine and my life was gone. He took it."

"Could you try to see him again?"

Trixie sipped her coffee.

"He died five years ago."

"I'm so sorry. So, so sorry."

Trixie pushed away her cup.

"Would you come somewhere with me?"

"Sure. Where?"

"Every once in a while, I go out to his grave. To talk to him. I'd like it if you came with me. It's only fifteen minutes away."

"Of course. Let's go."

"I'll drive."

Trixie drove to St. Adalbert's cemetery on South Sixth Street. It started to drizzle. There were no other mourners in sight when they pulled into the cemetery. Audrey followed Trixie across the grass to a small gravestone set back from the road. It said "Robert Paul." A picture of a Harley was etched on one side of the name and a bent fishing pole with a fish on the hook was etched on the other.

Audrey stood with her head bowed, hands clasped in front of her. Trixie approached the grave. Suddenly, she screamed.

"How's that working out for you, asshole?"

Audrey had her gun half-drawn before she stopped.

"That's all," Trixie said. "Let's go back to the Serb."

Trixie's eyes were wet as they drove away. A single tear fell down her cheek.

"I need some wine, girl. You with me?"

"I'm with you. You know it."

Chapter Sixty-Three

There were only a few people in the ballroom when Audrey and Trixie walked in. Trixie scowled as she looked around.

"It's early. But usually there's a few more by now. Oh, no!"

"What's the matter?"

"We're dead. Toast."

"Why?"

"See that guy over there?"

She pointed to a plump man in his sixties with an extremely large head and pale blue eyes. He wore his pants almost up to his nipples, with the belt fastened about six inches higher than normal. He stood by himself, head slightly tilted down, but his eyes strained up to peer around the room.

"That's Henry Linzmeyer. He lives with his mother. He hangs around politics. It's over. Stick a fork in me. I'm done."

"Trixie! What do you mean?"

"There was this old-age home in Pennsylvania? And there was this cat? The cat would walk into a resident's room and jump up on the bed a few hours before they died. The cat knew. Even if they weren't sick."

"Yeah, and?"

"Henry's the campaign cat. When he shows up early on election night, the candidate's a dead man walking. Every time. He knows."

Audrey laughed.

"Trixie! That's superstitious."

"Yeah? The cat knows. And stay away from him. You think you've seen strange in this town? You ain't seen nothing."

"When do things start? When do Bernie and Joe get here?"

"Polls close at eight. Jimmy and the Webers will get here a little before that. You see those guys over there?"

A half dozen men were sitting on folding chairs in the corner. Each was working a phone. No one paid the slightest attention to anyone else.

"Government relations," said Trixie. "Lobbyists. That's the rat patrol. They sniff around at elections. They start with the incumbent. The stations broadcast the exit polls a minute after they close. If the exits are bad, the rat patrol scurries down the gangplank to get to the other guy. If they're good, they come shining around the candidate. You know you lost if those chairs are empty."

Trixie took a call. Audrey walked over to the coffee urns. As she filled her cup, Henry Linzmeyer walked over and stood a foot away from her. His enormous head was tilted down. His chin hung down almost to his belt, which was fastened just under his armpits. He peered up at her without speaking.

"Hi, I'm Henry," he said.

He didn't extend his hand.

"Oh, hi. I'm Audrey."

He looked her over.

"I got circumcised last week," Henry said.

"You did? How, I mean, I hope it went all right."

"Excellent. It went excellent."

"Congratulations. But please excuse me. I have to step out to take a call."

Frannie, Bernie, and I got to Serb Hall at seven-thirty. Jerry Piano and Terry were sitting at the bar in the corner, knocking a few down. Jimmy Fieblewicz was roaming through the crowd, thanking people for coming.

There were tables with baskets of pretzels and popcorn set all over the room. Fannie and I sat down. I snarfed a handful of popcorn. Bernie went over to get a soda. Four TV sets were mounted in the front, each covering a different station. The CBS, NBC and Fox affiliates ran their regular programming until the polls closed. The ABC station, WISN Channel 12, broke in occasionally with updates.

"Good evening. I'm Kathy Mykleby with an update on this election shortly before the polls close. There's been a record-high voter turnout for municipal elections. We're especially following the Fifth Aldermanic District race, where incumbent Jimmy Fieblewicz is being challenged by community activist, Santiago Flores."

"What?"

Trixie yelled at the camera.

"Active doing what?"

"And we go now to Colleen Henry, reporting live from Oklahoma Avenue School, where the polls close in twenty-five minutes. Colleen?"

"Thanks, Kathy. Voter turnout in the Fifth Aldermanic has been heavy. A poll worker here told me that it's running ten percent above normal. He told me that it's also heavy in the other precincts in the Fifth Aldermanic District."

"Did he say why they think that's happening?"

"He said it's due to heavier-than-normal turnout among Latino voters, Kathy."

"Thanks, Colleen. Stay tuned to WISN Channel 12 for the election results right when the polls close at eight o'clock."

Audrey Knapp walked over to Bernie.

"Can I talk to you, Bernie?"

"Sure."

They sat down at an empty table in the corner.

"What are your plans, Bernie?"

"Finish school and that. I don't know."

"You have a lot of ability. Does your mom like math, too?"

"Not really. She's supersmart, but she likes different stuff."

"Your dad does though, right?"

"Yeah."

"Is he going to be okay?"

"Yeah."

"Do you feel sad sometimes, Bernie? About your dad?"

"Kind of."

She handed him a card.

"Let me know what you're thinking of doing when you get out of college. Please call me anytime. Even if you just want to talk."

"Thanks."

He took the card.

"But I don't want to work for you. I mean not for you. For, you know, spies and such."

"I know. I don't want you to either, Bernie. It's not a good life. You're always in a strange city by yourself. You don't have family and friends. Not like you do."

"Yeah."

Audrey stood up.

"Can I give you a hug?"

"Yeah."

He hugged her tightly back.

The crowd had gotten much larger. There weren't many real smiles. You could feel the tension just before the verdict.

Audrey Knapp walked over to our table. Jerry and Terry had joined us.

"I've come to say goodbye," Audrey said.

"We're kind of getting used to you," Jerry said.

There was a commotion in the back of the room.

"Gangs!" yelled Henry Linzmeyer.

He pointed to the back.

"The gangs are coming!"

Jerry Piano stood up. A dozen young Latino men in Levi jackets walked up front. A few wore durags. They started to hand out leaflets. Hector Gallego waved at Jerry.

"What the hell you doing here?" Jerry said.

"Politics, man. I'm running for County Board. Same streets as the Fifth Aldermanic, man."

"So?"

"Heard there was political action here. I'm droppin' lit."

Trixie came running over.

"What's up?"

"Droppin' lit."

"Hector's a county board candidate next spring," Jerry said. "And he's helped me out."

"Let me see it."

Hector handed Trixie a leaflet. It had an unflattering picture of a man who was stepping off a curb, with one leg in the air. He was scowling. His skin was mottled.

"Who's that?"

"The incumbent. No good. Got to take him out."

Trixie kept reading.

"Well, first thing, you want to go light negative in the beginning. This is too heavy. It says here, 'How much money is missing from the County Board, and what did this man know about it?'"

"Right."

"I hadn't heard there was money missing."

"Who knows? I'm only asking."

"Trixie, there's your next candidate," said Audrey.

Hector's eyes sparkled.

"You represent me?"

Music suddenly rang out from the TVs. Each set cut to its anchor desk.

"Good evening. This is Kathy Mykleby of WISN Channel 12 with full election results. We can now report that exit polls in the Fifth Aldermanic District show a surprising upset of incumbent Jimmy Fieblewicz. Our exit polls show that challenger Santiago Flores will defeat the incumbent sixty-eight percent to thirty-two percent. We now go live to the campaign headquarters of Santiago Flores. Colleen Henry is with his campaign spokesman, Bautista Fragoso, who will be Alderman Flores's Chief of Staff. Colleen, can you . . .?"

The crowd groaned. I put my arm around Jimmy. As the raw numbers started to scroll at the bottom of the screen, I saw Audrey walk to the side door by the empty chairs where the lobbyists had been sitting. She opened the door and stepped out into the night.

About the Author

Matthew J. Flynn is a prominent lawyer, politician, and former Naval Officer. His career in politics and service in the Navy have given him an insight into how our government and our enemies operate. He uses this perspective as an inspiration for his thrillers. Flynn lives with his wife in Milwaukee.

Upcoming New Release!

HUNTING BERNIE WEBER
BERNIE WEBER: MATH GENIUS SERIES
BOOK 3
BY
MATTHEW J. FLYNN

Our math genius, Bernie Weber, is a high school student in Milwaukee who has the ability to deduce the prime factors of any large number. (FYI: modern cryptology is based on using large prime numbers, which computers cannot extract when they are used in encoded messages).

When Bernie performs as "Pryme Knumber" in a math circus at a Milwaukee college, an intelligence officer in the audience realizes the value of his innate ability and informs the CIA of this potential human resource. They test Bernie to see if his ability is authentic and decide to give him a thumb drive with an encoded message to crack. By mistake, they give him a top-secret message they have intercepted but have not been able to decipher....

For more information
visit: www.SpeakingVolumes.us

Now Available!

MILWAUKEE JIHAD
BERNIE WEBER: MATH GENIUS SERIES
BOOK 1
BY
MATTHEW J. FLYNN

**For more information
visit:** www.SpeakingVolumes.us

Now Available!

MATT SCOTT'S
SURVIVING THE LION'S DEN SERIES
BOOKS 1 – 2

 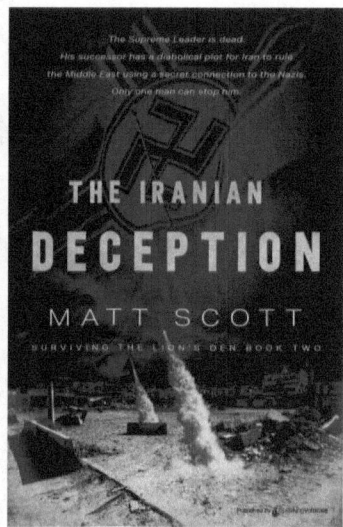

For more information
visit: www.SpeakingVolumes.us

Now Available!

STEPHEN STEELE'S
THE TROUBLE WITH MIRACLES
BOOKS 1 – 3

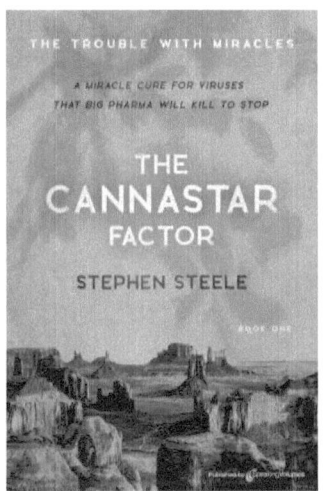

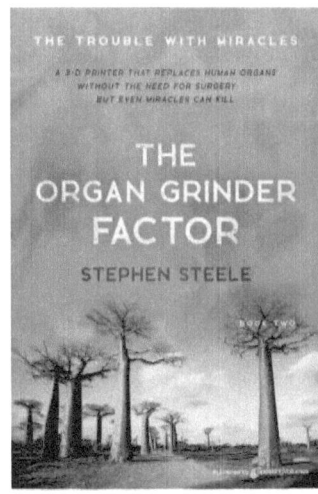

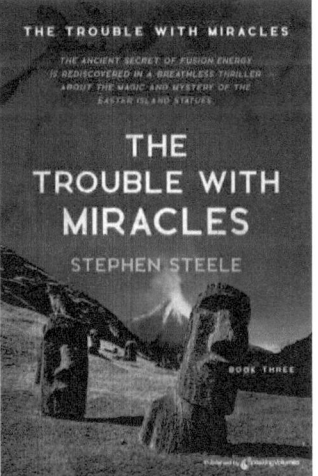

**For more information
visit:** www.SpeakingVolumes.us